DEVILISH DEALS

DEVILISH DEALS

EDITED BY JONATHAN W. THURSTON-TORRES

A THURSTON HOWL PUBLICATIONS BOOK

CONTENTS

IN THE DETAILS
SCOTT HUGHES

"I'm begging," said the balding, pudgy man close to tears as he dropped to his knees and clung to the flowing crimson cape of the demonic figure towering over him. "I've spent years, *decades* trying to finish my novel, and it's all... shit." The tears spilled out in a blubbering tsunami as he spoke this last word, contorting it into a multisyllabic *shi-iii-iii-iii-iii-t.*

With his bright red hands, the looming demon tugged his cape from the man's grip, rolled his fiery eyes, and sighed.

"Unholy fuck," the demon muttered in a deep and gravely yet aloof voice. "Don't you realize what a goddamn cliché we're both in right now?"

The man let out a final bleat and peered up at the demon, confused. He wiped a shiny trail of yellowish snot from his nostril. "What?"

"You're... Well, you're supposed to be, or desire to be, a writer, right... uh..." He snapped his red fingers a few times until the man realized the demon was trying to recall his name.

"George," the man said.

"George, yeah. The first thing a writer should learn is to avoid clichés, and here you are fucking smack dab in the middle of one of your own doing. I mean, look at this."

He gestured to their surroundings, and George, still on his knees, blinked stupidly at the six-foot pentagram he'd drawn on his living room floor in pig's blood, the lit black candles at each point of the star, and the goat entrails encircling the whole necromantic scene.

"It's what the book said to do," said George.

The demon grunted. "Come on, Georgie Boy. A book? What fucking book? One you found in the dusty attic of an old bookstore locked in a box with the words *DO NOT OPEN* carved into the wood? Or, wait, let me guess..."

He scratched his pointed goatee with black fingernails. And, yes, he realized how hackneyed his own appearance was: red skin, pointed ears, black beard, crimson clothes and cape... goddamn horns jutting from his forehead. That wasn't his fault. His form was always dictated by whomever had summoned him—whatever their concept of the Devil was. To some, he looked as he did now, like something from a 50s B-movie. To some, he was the fallen angel: an androgynous white-robed, dove-winged being. He hated that one because underneath the toga-like robes, he had no genitalia. He'd occasionally been a woman, sometimes wretched and disfigured, sometimes enchanting and sensuous—*bewitching*, you might say—which was interesting if not enjoyable. He'd been animals: a serpent, a goat, a jackal, a bat. He'd been bizarre animal hybrids: a wolf with a snake's head, a snake with a wolf's head, a creature with both a snake's head *and* wolf's head. He'd been a twelve-foot-tall bat-winged beast with cloven hooves, matted fur, and a maw full of fangs. He'd been a tentacled eldritch monstrosity. He'd appeared in countless forms.

His favorite was when he was called forth by a woman in China in 1334. She was barren and wanted a child, so she'd conjured him as a nude muscular divine being with locks of shining sapphire hair, luminescent skin, and a cock like a glittering marble column. He fucked her and impregnated her, but as these things always went, her "child" was a demonic rat the size of a schnauzer that gnawed its way out of her womb and proceeded to spread the Black Death across Asia and Europe. What fun. Before the boredom of it all consumed him.

"Let's see..." he said to George. "When you had the idea to make a deal with the Devil, a distant uncle passed away and left you this mysterious book filled with ancient spells and curses. Hmm?"

"No, I... I found it in the occult section of the library."

"Oh, for fuck's sake." He rapped his red knuckles on George's forehead. "Anyone in there? I'm the fucking Devil, not a cheesecake recipe or some factoid for a research paper. *The fucking Devil.* All you need to do is say, 'Hey, Devil, I'd like to talk,' and bam! There I am."

"I was—"

"Forget it. Let's get this show on the road. Stand up. Come on, get to your feet."

George stood.

"You want to make a deal with me to write an amazing novel, right?" the Devil asked.

George nodded.

"And you know how this goes? You're a 'writer.'" He made air quotes with his red fingers. "I hope you've fucking read *Doctor Faustus.*"

George blinked dumbly.

"*Faust? The Devil and Daniel Webster?* 'The Devil and Tom Walker'?"

George shook his head.

"Fuck, at least tell me you've seen *The Devil's Advocate.* Al Pacino and Keanu Reeves?" The Devil imitated Pacino from the film—perfectly, of course: "'Let me give you a little inside information about God. God likes to watch. He's a prankster.'"

Again, George shook his head.

The Devil covered his face and groaned. "Well, Georgie Porgie, no wonder you can't write for shit. You don't fucking read anything, or even watch movies apparently." He dropped his hands. "All right, so the way this goes is that I give you what you wish for, but that leads to something ironically horrible... or horribly ironic, usually directly to you." He tapped the end of George's nose with a black-nailed finger. "In your case, asking for a renowned novel, I'd say..."—he gestured in small circles with both hands—"...you'll get mauled by a bear and barely survive or die in a freak accident like getting hit by a meteorite, which will stir public interest in 'your' book." He did air quotes again for the word *your.* "Still up for it, Georgie?"

The man had been gaping cluelessly as though he had stumbled into the current situation by happenstance instead of setting this whole ordeal in motion himself by summoning Satan with pig's blood, goat entrails, a pentagram, black candles, and some rinky-dink spell from a library book. Then he stood up straighter and for the first time donned an expression of dark determination instead of whimpering cowardice and stupidity.

He nodded. "Yes."

The Devil narrowed his fiery eyes. "Really? Like, *really*? Knowing you're going to spontaneously combust or get fucked to death by a lion that escapes from a zoo?"

George got a little fire in his own eyes. "You're goddamn right."

The Devil couldn't help tossing back his head and laughing. "Throwing out the big GD, huh? You might be my kinda guy after all, Georgie. So, do you fancy a Stephen King style best seller or some Steinbeck literary masterpiece?" The man didn't have to answer. The smirk tugging at the corner of his lips said everything. The Devil grinned. "Of course. The moneymaker, not the pretentious academic cat piss."

George nodded.

"Genre?" the Devil asked. "Mystery? Horror? Science Fiction? Surely not romance."

"Horror."

"Horror, right. You did summon the Prince of Darkness, after all. So be it."

He clapped his red hands together, causing George to flinch, and sparks flew from his palms. When he separated his hands, a roll of parchment formed from thin air, sizzling and smoking, like a video of a scroll burning to ash playing in reverse.

The Devil unrolled the paper and presented it. "Read carefully, please."

George snatched it, and his eyes darted from one line to the next. After the man's earlier confession, the Devil knew George couldn't be reading too closely. They never did.

George's eyes left the parchment and met the Devil's with the same giddy avarice that everyone's always had, a look that said, *Where do I sign?*

While George had been reading, the Devil had produced a quill—yeah, yeah, how cliché—which he now held out. The man greedily grabbed it, like a starving person would a scrap of meat, and tried scratching it across the bottom of the parchment.

He looked up. "There's no ink."

"Ink, Georgie?" The Devil furrowed his red brow and shook his head ever so slightly. "This isn't some extended warranty for a Honda Civic. Blood, my dear man. *Your* blood."

George eyed the quill's point, then handed the contract to the Devil to hold momentarily. The Devil watched him with a blank expression, bored by the unnecessary theatrics of it all. Why did it have to be this way? Why did it have to be so elaborate, so serious, so utterly ritualistic? If it were up to him, he'd settle it with a handshake. Hell, a simple nod and *thank you* would suffice. No, if it were truly up to him, he'd slap the ever-living shit out of these people and tell them to just do whatever the fuck they had summoned him to do for them, the sad sack motherfuckers, and if they couldn't, then they should get the hell over it and get on with their lives.

George jabbed the quill into his thumb, winced, and pulled it out, the tip wet with his blood. The Devil handed back the parchment, and George sloppily smeared his punctured digit on it as he signed his name with the other hand. When he finished, the Devil took the contract and quill, rolled the parchment around the feather, and—with no pizzazz or showmanship whatsoever—made them disappear like the most lackluster street magician using sleight of hand to vanish a watch into thin air. Then once more he slapped his sparking palms together, and when he parted them this time, a loose manuscript of a few hundred pages unburned into existence.

As soon as it materialized, George seized it with both hands—smearing blood on it as he had the contract—and, eyes as wide as full moons, read aloud what was typed on the first page.

"*The Rot* by George Boyle." He glanced up at the Devil.

"What's it about?"

"For fuck's sake, Georgie Porgie, you at least have to read *this* book."

"Thank you, thank you, thank you!"

As always, they immediately forgot their part of the bargain. "Thank me, sure. Let's see if you're thanking me when a sinkhole swallows your entire house with you in it."

George wasn't paying him attention. He was flipping through the pages of "his" best-selling book. Once they got what they desired, it was like he didn't exist anymore.

"Will you clean all this shit up?" the Devil said, motioning to the mess on the floor. "I'd prefer if no one knew I was involved. Hey, George!" He smacked the side of the man's head. George looked at him in shock, as though he hadn't spent the last fifteen minutes making a deal with Satan. "Clean. This. Shit. Up."

George nodded, his pudgy neck waddles jiggling. "Yeah, sure." The fucker then actually turned away, plopped himself cross-legged right in the blood and entrails, and continued reading the manuscript.

"Goddamn humans," the Devil mumbled before closing his blazing eyes and vanishing in a burst of flames that George didn't notice.

George died, of course, soon after. He contracted a never-before-seen type of leprosy from the wound on this thumb and succumbed, after suffering quite horrifically in a sealed-off quarantine room of a hospital, a few weeks later. The story surrounding his death, however, drummed up interest in his novel about a flesh-eating virus that takes over the world he had repeatedly mentioned to his doctors and nurses. This made the local, then national news, and after a bidding war, *The Rot* was published the next year by Simon & Schuster. Stephen King actually wrote a blurb for the cover. In its first week, it sold nearly half a million copies, and more its second week—and even more its third week. As promised, it became a number-one best seller, and remained on the best-seller charts of the *New York Times* and Amazon, among others, for over a year. A famous actor that even George would've recognized did the audio book, and the film adaptation raked in quite a haul at the box office.

The Rot made millions—although, as the contract stated clearly if he'd read closely enough, Georgie Porgie never saw one cent of that since he was, alas, dead.

That's how it always went. They never read the fine print.

A lot of people wanted dead loved ones back. Spouses, kids, parents, siblings, friends, even pets. Those were easy. They came back zombified. Duh. Many guys asked for bigger cocks, more sex, or both. Also easy. They fucked until they caught a disease that rotted their dicks off. If they requested a huge cock but didn't explicitly say anything about sex, the Devil would sneak a clause into the contract that made them impotent. Give them a giant member that did nothing except dangle like a wet rag.

They never ever read the fine print.

One time, there was a former child actress from a well-known kids' TV show who couldn't get roles as an adult. After her deal, she landed a role in Scorsese's latest movie and gave a riveting performance as a drug addict although she went a little too method and ended up OD'ing before the film premiered and posthumously won, among several acting awards, an Oscar.

For about sixty percent of people, it was something career and/or money related (often involving fame like good ole Georgie), thirty-five percent wanted something relationship/family/sex related, and five percent was... other. Like this one guy who wished for the perfect cheeseburger. That's it. Too bad he choked to death on the last bite. He did die smiling.

Yet no one, not a single person, ever read the fine print. The details. Even though that's where everyone always says the Devil is, for fuck's sake.

And after each deal, the Devil would return here, where he is now, to this colorless, shapeless, timeless liminal space with only his thoughts. What he wouldn't give to get himself out of this ceaseless monotonous nightmare of making ironically cliché deals with humans...

Wait. Wait, wait, wait, wait, *wait*. Why couldn't he?

Yes... Yes, of course he could. As he had told George, all he had to do was ask.

"Hey," says the Devil. "Hey you."

Silence.

He clears his throat, then speaks again. "I said, 'Hey you'! Yes, *you*. Scott Hughes. The person who is writing... will write... has written—whatever, it's all the same... The person writing this. Go ahead. Type. Answer me."

I stop typing and stare at the blinking cursor line on the screen in Microsoft Word. Had I just typed my own name—addressed myself—in this story? It didn't feel like I did—it felt like someone else had—yet there it was all the same.

"Well," says the Devil, "you kinda sorta did... and you didn't. Writers—creators of any kind—are simultaneously in control of their creations and totally not in control of them. So, you did and you didn't, Scott."

I'm not drunk or high. Could this be an acid flashback from high school?

"No, you're not having a flashback," says the Devil. "You did acid once when you were sixteen. You're not Keith Richards. You're having a conversation with me. There are others here too, people reading this—I can sense them—but they can't speak to me here. Only you can."

That's it. My brain is snapping. I've got to delete this document and—

"No, no," says the Devil. "None of that. Let's just chat. Go ahead. Try it. Tell me hello."

My fingers hover over the keys.

"Come on," he says. "Clickety clack. H-E-L-L... O."

Hello.

"There you go!" he says. "Now, was that so hard?"

I guess not, but... this is weird. *Super* weird. Like, what the actual fuck is happening right now?

"Scott, you and I are having a conversation."

I'm having a conversation. With the Devil. With a character. In a story I'm writing.

"Well, yes and no, as I said before. Creators are both in control and not in control of their work. Although it seems to you that you are writing this in the moment, the truth—the bigger Truth with a capital T—is that it also *hasn't* been written yet and it already *has been* written."

Uh...

"Okay, it's like this: To you, you are currently writing the story, and it's not finished yet so there's still some left to be written. To your readers, they've got the whole thing in front of them, so it's already written. Hell, they might be reading this years or decades after you're dead."

I think my brain's going to melt.

"Nah, you'll be fine, Scott. Enough of that. We've got business to get to, all right?"

Okay...

"I'd like to make a deal with you."

You, the Devil, want to make a deal with me?

"Right."

But you're just a character.

"That's where you're wrong, Scooter. You've conjured me here in your story as opposed to your living room. I'm still the Devil. Still real."

I don't know if—

"Look, I don't care if you believe me. You can discuss that with your therapist. Will you make a deal with me or what?"

I don't want anything.

"For fuck's sake. It's for *me*. In this case, you're playing the part of me, and I'm the sad sack motherfucker asking for something despite knowing it'll have some ironic twist. So, will you do it, Scott?"

Hypothetically, let's say I will. What do you want?

"For you to write me out of existence."

What? I can't do that. Even if I wanted to, I don't think I *could*.

"Of course you can. You killed ole Georgie a few pages ago

no problem."

I didn't kill him.

"Well, you did and you didn't. What's important here is that you *can*. You wrote me into existence in this story, so you can just as easily write me out. So, Scott, what do you say?"

I lean back from my laptop and look around my living room as if the answer is there somewhere. All that's here—besides my laptop and furniture—is my deaf fourteen-year-old shih tzu, Pip, lying on his side asleep and my two-year-old beagle, Bowie, eyeing me curiously with his head cocked.

"Hey!" says the Devil. "You're not going to think about this for eternity, are you? I've got that long. You, however, do not."

Okay. If this is merely another story that's veered into Metaville, so be it. If this is me going crazy, so be it. If this is me truly communicating with Satan, so be it.

My hands return to the keyboard.

All right. What do I need to do?

"Fan-fucking-tastic!" says the Devil. "All you have to do is create a contract for me to sign, like I've created for all those people throughout the ages. One that states I will cease to exist."

I don't know how to write a contract. I'd have to research it. It could take days. *Weeks*.

"Aw, come on now, Scott. You're starting to sound like Georgie Porgie. You're a fiction writer. You don't have to write the whole fucking contract line-by-line. You simply need to *describe* it, just enough for me to know—and the readers to be able to imagine—what's in it. You've already done that with George. Well, I did that too."

We both did it. Together. I get it now.

"Then do it."

A roll of parchment forms from thin air, sizzling and smoking, like a video of a scroll burning to ash playing in reverse.

"Nice," he says.

The Devil, however you'd like to picture him, takes the

paper and unrolls it.

Read carefully, please.

"Ha fucking ha." As he reads over the contents, though, he begins to genuinely chuckle.

What?

"It's perfect."

Why's that?

"Well, there's a twist, of course. How deliciously evil."

What is it?

"I will become nonexistent, as I asked. However, each time somebody reads this, I will form into existence, doomed to repeat my dealings with Georgie Porgie. And with you."

Only when people read it.

"Yes, but because we're having this conversation right now—for the first time? the tenth time? the hundredth time? the hundred-thousandth? who knows?—I've been ripped from nonexistence again. You and I both know your sisters will read it. Hello, Carra and Libby. And your mom, she loves your stuff. Well, she loves *you*. She'll read it a few times. Hello, Jan. And you, you narcissistic bastard. You'll read this yourself twenty times at least. Hello, future Scott! And that's only you and a few people in your immediate family. Every time someone picks up this story, poof! Here I am." He sighs, though still sounds amused. "I couldn't have come up with a more devilish contract myself. Quill please."

A quill appears. The Devil takes it and pierces his skin—whatever type of skin you imagine he has—with the tip, then signs the bottom of the scroll. He exhales with an almost sexual pleasure as the parchment and quill burn away.

"All right," he says. "I'm ready. Until, you know, somebody reads this."

Okay. Here we—

"One more thing."

Yeah?

"Making this deal with me… In this scenario, you're the Devil."

Yeah, you said that already.

"What I mean is, you're cursed. Like I was. Like I am. Like I will be."

How so?

"Anytime someone reads this, I'll live again. I'll have to make the deal with Georgie Porgie. I'll do all this over and over and over with him. And with you."

Yeah...

"Well, people will likely read this after you die. You, the real you out there wherever, could already be dead right now, yet you're here in this story talking to me."

I don't follow.

"That contract I signed? That deal we made? The same punishment you inflicted on me, you've inflicted on yourself. Whenever people read this, I'll be reawakened into existence, as will you. In the details. That's where they say I am. And now we both literally will be."

I stop typing and sit back on my couch, staring at the laptop screen.

"Oh, fuck it," says the Devil. "I don't give a shit if you understand it now. You'll get it eventually when you read this for the fiftieth time." He shakes his head, whatever you imagine his head to be—if he even has one. "I'm ready."

Okay. Here we go.

I type the sentence: The Devil ceases to exist.

I wait.

Hello?

No answer.

To be sure he's really gone, I try speaking aloud as well as typing all the names for him I know: Devil, Satan, Lucifer, Beelzebub, Prince of Darkness. Then I Google "different names for the Devil" and speak and type those to ensure I don't miss any: Abaddon, Ahriman, Angel of Light, Angra Mainyu, Apollyon, Ba'al Zabul, Belial, El Diablo, Erlik, Fallen Star, Father of Lies, Great Red Dragon, Hades, Iblis, King of the Bottomless Pit, Lord of Darkness, Mastema, Mephistopheles, Old Scratch, Samael, Satanael, Sathariel, Serpent of Old, Shaitan, and a hundred others. I try them all.

Still no answer.

So, here I am. Just me and my story.

And you.

You, whoever you are, have conjured me into existence. Read this again sometime. Tell a friend to read it. Tell a few. Bring me back. That way, I won't ever die.

And that's not such a bad deal, is it? Not so bad at all.

THE ETERNAL GIFT
JAY BOWER

Ash Heidle curled around the corner of the brick building. Dark shadows danced in the alley ahead of him. The soft glow of the sulfuric streetlights didn't stretch across the entire street, leaving a swath of darkness like a barrier he shouldn't cross. Steam rose from the utility access covers in the streets.

He swallowed hard. It was then or never. He'd sought those people for months. That was where they said to meet, a dead-end alley tucked between Olive and Locust Streets in downtown St. Louis. Originally, he assumed he read the message wrong, but no, that was the place. He was told a red door held his destiny. A bead of sweat ran down his forehead as he stared at the door.

It was time.

Shoving the growing alarm in his head to a dark place within, he straightened his thick winter coat and strode confidently toward the door.

Ash knocked three times as instructed, his knuckles stinging on the metal door. A small slit slid to the side and dark eyes peered out at him.

"Name?" the gruff voice said.

"Heidle. Ah…Ash Heidle," he said, correcting himself. If done incorrectly, they warned him he'd be turned away. That was the last thing he wanted.

The slider slammed closed and a series of locks were unlocked and the door pulled inward. "Come on," the man said, though more like a butler greeting a distinguished guest.

When Ash accidentally stumbled on the video game Hell's Portal, he followed what he assumed to be a joke through countless clicks, navigating their secretive website until he unlocked a portal granting him access to the Keeper of Hell himself. At least that's what the guy called himself. Playing along, Ash soon found the guy charming and not as crazy as he originally assumed. The longer he chatted with him, the more he believed what he said was true: they'd found a gateway to Hell and true immortality as the new King of Hell, the ultimate prize. All he had to do was offer a sacrifice opening the portal and…survive.

Stepping inside the red door, Ash's destiny awaited.

"Hurry in," the man at the door said. Standing about six and a half feet tall and nearly as wide, his hands looked as though they'd crush boulders.

The entry hallway was dimly lit with a red bulb. The walls and floor were all red. Ash didn't know if he should laugh at the crude attempt to mimic hell or worry that something terrible was soon to happen.

The man pushed past him and stalked down a hallway, turning back to Ash. "Come on before His Darkness decides you aren't worthy of The Gift."

Ash followed, turning the corner behind the man.

Then reality set it. They entered a large room painted black. A single red lightbulb blazed overhead. Four women and one man in red robes with a black rope tied around their waists stood on the other side of a metal table where a young woman was tied down with the same black rope. She was nude and had a gag shoved in her mouth. Turning her head toward him, tears ran down her cheek. She fought against her restraints and tried screaming through the gag to no use.

"Ash?" the robed man said. He stepped away from the rest. His shaved head glowed red from the light. The mans dark eyes sent a chill down Ash's spine. His voice was calm.

"Welcome to the ceremony. You are ready, are you not?"

He stepped closer and Ash's heart thundered in his chest.

"I am," he replied. He'd built up to this moment, practicing on small animals to the point he no longer cared to take a life. Though staring at the girl on the table, he wondered if he could follow through with the ritual. It was the only way to enter

Hell.

"I am the Keeper. Truly honored to finally meet you." The Keeper extended his hand and Ash shook it. "We have little time to wait. The Gift is ready. All you must do is claim it." He pulled a large knife from his robe and handed it to him. Ash inspected it. Bone handled with a six-inch blade sharpened so that it glistened in the red light. It was what it was to get him into the game.

The Keeper ushered him closer to the girl, whose eyes widened at the sight of the knife. She struggled against the bindings. The four women each took a position near her hands and feet as guardians against her escape.

On the far side of the room, Ash noticed a chair similar to what he'd seen in beauty shops to dry hair, though the headpiece was far more menacing with cables and wires running down from it to the seat itself. He followed the path of a cable on the floor that ran to the table and up toward a drain. *Not a cable, a pipe.* It's where the blood flowed from the sacrifice to the system, unlocking his access.

"It is time," the Keeper said. Ash had wondered what it would feel like at this moment as he stood on the precipice of Hell. Thrilling. Exhilarating. Sickening. Still, he stepped forward. It was what he wanted.

Standing next to the girl, the Keeper began chanting in Latin.

"Magister, obsecro noster accipere donum."

Sweat poured down Ash's back. The Keeper continued the chant.

"Magister, obsecro noster accipere donum."

Veins bulged on the girl's neck.

"Magister, obsecro noster accipere donum."

Ash lowered himself, bringing the blade's edge to her soft skin along her belly. She screamed through the gag, but he could think of nothing other than entering Hell.

"Magister, obsecro noster accipere donum."

Slowly Ash drew the blade across her stomach, a red line following behind it. The girl struggled, but the women made sure she was secure. Ash inserted his blade into her soft skin and dragged it through her flesh, opening another large gash. Blood poured down her waist and onto the metal table. A small stream flowed toward the drain. The process had begun.

The Keeper continued to chant and Ash, lost in his work, continued to cut the girl's flesh. He wondered how much blood he needed before the portal opened. He knew slicing her throat would give him the most blood the fastest, but would also kill her quicker. The Keeper had instructed him to keep her alive as long as possible to gain the most amount of blood. It was what Ash practiced with all those animals.

The headpiece on the chair flickered briefly.

"Should I stop?" Ash asked.

"Continue. You don't have enough yet," The Keeper said.

The four women chanted the words of the Keeper.

"Magister, obsecro noster accipere donum." Their delicate voices bolstered Ash.

He gashed her fair skin. Streaks of red crossed her body. He saw her not as an object of sex, but as the way to immortality.

The four women chanted softly. The headpiece flickered several times as though an engine trying to start.

"It is time," the Keeper said at last. "Finish the ceremony and enter your destiny."

Ash looked the girl in her eyes, her fear fully exposed. "Thank you for your gift," he whispered. Slicing the blade across her throat, blood spilled out. More than all the cuts he made to that point. He stood back and watched the blood run toward the drain.

Across the room, the headpiece flickered wildly. Red and white flashes of light alternated like a wicked strobe light.

"Come, the time is now," the Keeper said. Ash carefully set the knife down on the metal table. The Keeper put a hand on his back and ushered him to the chair.

Ash wanted to cry. Overjoyed at his fortune, he turned to the Keeper.

"Thank you," he breathed.

"You will be one of us soon. You have done well," the Keeper said. He tilted the headpiece back so Ash could get in the seat. Once settled in, the Keeper bent to look him in the eye.

"I wish you strength through your ordeal," he said.

"Thank you for everything," Ash replied.

The Keeper lowered the headpiece. Ash's heart pounded harder in his chest as a calming silence fell over him in the device's darkness. He breathed in slowly, trying to settle himself. Soon his body was back under control.

A small pinpoint of red light appeared in the black void ahead. *There it is! I've made it*, he thought.

A moment of silence, calm and soothing followed.

Then the light exploded, engulfing him in flames. The screams of thousands of dead souls surrounded him, each crying out for mercy. Horrific and painful, he could do nothing to stop their agony or protect himself from their cries. Screaming, howling, tortured souls called out to him in the flames.

The flames imploded and the screams abruptly stopped, their echoes lingering in his head.

"Welcome to Hell," a deep voice said, startling him. He turned to the left, and that's when he realized he stood within a dark cavern illuminated by a reddish glow, though he could see no source for the light.

Standing next to him was a demon. Red skin, black hair, charcoal eyes. The demon wore thick black pants but no shirt, his rippling muscles exposed for all to see.

"It worked," Ash muttered.

"Indeed it has. Did you think otherwise?" the demon asked. His deep voice rumbled within Ash's chest.

When Ash bought into the realization that he could take over Hell by beating what amounted to a video game, he leapt at the chance. He'd played games his entire life. Why not find immortality within one? If nothing else, the virtual experience would be worth it. Though not for the sacrifice.

"How do I start? What are the rules of the game?" he

asked.

A grin slowly crept across the demon's face. "The rules? Hell has no rules."

"Sure you do. Every game has them."

"Of course. The sacrifice must come willingly. That is the only rule."

Ash thought about the girl, about her fearful expression, and wondered if she had voluntarily offered herself for his glory. He didn't know her at all. Why would she do such a thing?

The demon turned, and a path glowed red on the black ground. Without another word, the demon walked ahead.

Ash followed as the distant screams of the damned surrounded him. He'd need to get used to this if he were to become the new King of Hell. With nothing left to live for at home, this was his only chance to live forever. The bone cancer he'd been dealing with was a torture no twenty-three-year-old man should endure. Fuck life. Fuck living. This was his reality now.

They marched in silence for a long time until they crested a small hill overlooking a deep pit with a solid onyx obelisk in the center.

"There," the demon said, pointing at it. "It all happens there."

"Great, I wanna start my first quest."

The demon led him to the obelisk. As they neared the sleek black stone, Ash noticed a metal clasp just above head-height.

"What's that for?" Ash asked.

"It's how this all begins," the demon said.

"How?"

"Place your hands through the ring, then all will be revealed."

Ash hesitated, fearful that it was a trick of some sort.

"What happens if I don't?"

"Then you perish."

Going back to the living in that decrepit body wasn't appealing. Not existing anymore, not dealing with the pain…that was exquisite. But the lure of power called him. In this world, he could be something he never could before: relevant. It sealed it for him.

Turning his back to the obelisk, Ash placed his hands within the metal ring. The moment he did, flames erupted around the pit. The metal slammed tight around his wrists, immobilizing him. He struggled against the binding, but it wouldn't let go.

"You better not lie to me!" he yelled to the demon.

"You expect to come to Hell and what…be given the keys? Your kind grow weaker and dumber."

Ash screamed, realizing that maybe he made a mistake.

Behind the demon, a larger creature towered over him. Red-skinned, black hair, and with long black claws. It looked similar to the demon, but deadlier.

"Master," the demon said to the newcomer. "The Keeper has offered another soul."

"What? No! I'm here to play a game!" Ash cried.

The larger demon stepped forward, the smaller demon sliding out of his way. He bent closer and snorted fire from his nostrils, singeing Ash's brown hair.

"Your soul is mine," he said. Ash thought this must be the Devil himself, the Morning Star, the Prince of Darkness.

The Devil placed a hand on Ash's forehead and he felt an immediate sensation of heat. When the Devil pulled his hand back, a small stream of black mist followed. Ash felt a surge of agony flow through him. It was like it had touched every nerve with pain and his body writhed against it. He howled and cried for his release, but the Devil did nothing to ease the pain.

Staring down at Ash, the Devil spoke. "The willing sacrifice. The soul now mine for eternal damnation. The gift freely given." Then the Devil smiled. "I accept."

Flames raced up Ash's body. He screamed as they burned his flesh, searing into his muscles underneath, and bursting his eyes in a momentous, cataclysmic explosion.

The pain subsided and the blackness of blindness was replaced with the pit surrounding him. The Devil and the demon were gone. He fought with the binding, but it held firm.

Then, the flames returned and eviscerated his body once more until his eyes again burst. Blackness settled in, then the pit returned.

He had a moment to think he'd been stuck in a continuous loop, like a spawn-trap in a video game. The flames came back, torturing him all over again. He cried for mercy, but there was none. His world went black, and then it started once more. The flames. The pain. The bursting.

In the distance, he heard the cries of the damned and knew his voice was now added to that chorus. He dared to think he could find a shortcut to immortality and reign as the King of Hell. He cried out as the flames took him again, plunging him into darkness.

The pit reemerged. He waited, hopeful the torture was over, then it started again. Over and over it went.

He'd found his ever-lasting life, a game fit for the Devil.

THE DEVIL IN HIS PANTS
MATTHEW BARRON

The pressure in Jake's jeans hurt. He pulled his shirt down over his pants and wiped his sweaty palms on the cotton.

Megan straightened up from the counter and pulled the neck of her shirt up. Had he been staring? Her bra pushed her breasts up and together under her nametag.

"Can I help you?" she asked.

He looked up into her blue eyes. Were those long lashes natural, he wondered, or painted on somehow? His heart pounded against his chest.

Jake's high, raspy voice cracked as he spoke. He hated the sound of it. "Have you thought any more about going out tonight?"

Megan let her mouth hang open. "I can't tonight. There are people in line behind you. Do you need to take out some money?"

"No." He looked behind him at the line of people. One woman scowled, complaining about the line to a friend on her cell phone. "Wait," Jake said to Megan. "I'll take out fifty."

Her long fingers blurred across the keypad. She had his account number practically memorized.

"What about tomorrow?" Jake asked.

"This isn't a good time. Why didn't you call me?"

"The number you gave me doesn't work."

Megan wrote a phone number on his receipt. "I changed numbers," she said quietly. "Jake, I'm sure you're an alright guy, but you need to work on your approach. Call when I'm not working." She looked behind him and raised her voice. "Next."

He turned to leave. The people in line behind him breathed

a collective sigh of relief.

Jake normally wasn't able to approach girls so aggressively. He and Megan had gone to school together. The familiarity made talking to her easier.

The pressure in his crotch had subsided, but when he looked down, he found the bulge remained. Jake stopped in the restroom. Adjusting his member up made it less visible through his pants, but on thinking of Megan, the pain returned. He locked the stall door. In mere seconds, Jake wiped his shame off the plastic seat with some toilet paper and flushed it away.

Jake washed his hands and left with his pants loose and relaxed.

He gave one last look over his shoulder at Megan as he walked out the glass doors. Was this her real number, he wondered, or just a ruse to get rid of him?

A young girl in line at the post office wore short-shorts. Denim crept up her butt cleavage and left half moons of brown muscle hanging over the back of her thighs.

His pants tightened again, and Jake shouted down at his crotch. "Oh, come on!"

The girl gave him a confused, frightened look, and Jake turned toward the post office boxes.

Did other men have this problem? Women thought he was creepy, and premature erections weren't a turn on. If he could just get laid once, the problem might go away, but he was destined to die alone.

Jake's heart leapt with hope at the small brown package inside his mailbox. He'd been awaiting the final ingredient for over a month.

Jake threw the gnarled mandrake root into the food processor. It ground and buzzed violently. He feared the blades would break against the tough fiber, but the grinding subsided into an even hum, and he added the other ingredients.

Jake spread the resulting paste out on a cookie sheet. The mixture took forever to dry in the oven. Ready-made powder hadn't done anything. Making it all himself had to work.

A bar separated the living room from the kitchenette. The room was dark except for the circle of candles on the hardwood floor. Mounds of dirty laundry seemed to undulate in the flickering orange light.

What would his parents say if they saw him burning the homemade mélange in the center of the circle? They were good, God-fearing folk. He had done as they would do, prayed for help. None came.

This was just another kind of prayer. Within the flames was a slip of paper with the name of a different god.

Flame gave way to smoke and the smell of rotten eggs. His groin ached with anticipation.

He collapsed on his knees and waited. The stinky cloud obscured the candlelit room in a brown film.

He continued to sit.

After twenty minutes, Jake finally blew out the candles. He had spent all his money on a fool's hope.

A faint crunching froze Jake before a darkened candle. It sounded like rodents crawling through the walls. Something wormlike poked up through the blackened powder. The slender digits were tipped with polished fingernails. Hands pushed floor and ash aside.

A lithe body wound its way up through the hardwood. The mystery woman waved back and forth like a dancing cobra, or a belly dancer with no spine. Though her body swayed, her round breasts remained trained on Jake. The fullness of her face gave it a quality of youthful innocence. This quality was ruined when she opened her eyes. Where her eyeballs should be, tufts of curly hair sprouted from the sockets. Her nipples were eyes staring Jake in the face.

"Well?" The demoness said.

Jake stood speechless. Mouths in her palms breathed deeply of his nervous sweat.

"Trouble with the ladies?" she said.

"Yes," Jake said. "Women don't like me. I want women to like me."

One breast remained focused on his face. The other looked

down at his crotch. "A strapping boy like you?"

Jake thought he should be repulsed by the sight of her, but the dancing hips, the waving arms and the observing breasts aroused him.

She smiled, revealing shark-like teeth. "You like?"

Did she mean to have sex with him? He couldn't see any legs below her hips. If she had any, they were still below the floor, but certainly not in the apartment below. He wondered how a demon like that made love.

Her eye sockets stared blindly at the wall behind him. "What would you give for this?" she asked. "To have any woman you want?"

He had known this was coming. "I will give you my soul."

"But we already have that," she said.

"What do you mean?" Had the act of summoning her sealed his doom, or had they owned him from the start? Perhaps the fate of men's souls was preordained.

"What will you give?" she asked again.

"What do you want?" Jake said.

Her body waved back and forth while her breasts gazed into him in silence.

"I'll give you anything!"

She smiled and grabbed his shoulder. The mouth in her hand bit into his flesh.

She pressed her other hand violently against his crotch. His lungs seized. Jake instantly had something like a dry orgasm and fell to the floor.

The whine of the smoke detector woke Jake. His shoulder was intact, not even sore. He touched his crotch and found it soft and healthy. He turned off the alarm, opened a window and got a fan to blow the fetid air out.

A tiny pile of smoldering ash remained in the center of the circle, but the floor was solid. Had it all been in his mind?

All he could think about was Megan.

He didn't even put on a jacket before running out of the apartment and into the night. A couple made out on a park bench. The girl pushed her date away and stared at Jake as he passed.

He must have looked a sight. He sniffed his t-shirt and found he was still covered in that sulfurous smell.

He buzzed the outer door of Megan's building, a large house that had been partitioned into apartments. She wasn't home, of course. It was Friday night and someone like her obviously had plans.

He sat on her front stoop and exhaled. Jake let his head rest on his arm. He hadn't realized how exhausted he had been.

"It's someone I know from school."

Jake awoke with hard cement jabbing into his back. Megan stood over him with a well-dressed man at her side. What a fool Jake had been! Sleeping on her stoop like a bum, smelling of sweat and sulfur! And there she was, fresh from her date, more beautiful than he had ever seen her. The man on her arm could have been a model.

"You want me to talk to him?" her date said.

"Go home," Megan said. "I'll handle him."

"You want me to leave you with him out here?"

"I've got it," she insisted. "Call me tomorrow."

"I don't like it," he protested once more. "This is weird!"

"Just go!"

The man scowled at Jake and walked slowly away. The man had, no doubt, imagined the date ending very differently.

Megan's eyes softened.

"I was out for a jog," Jake said. "I just sat down for a minute. I didn't realize where I was. I'm leaving."

"No!" She said. "You look exhausted. Why don't you come up for a drink? It will get your energy back up."

Jake couldn't believe his ears.

She led him by the hand into the interior hallway. Once through her apartment door, she tossed down her purse. Without a word, she pressed against him. Her soft lips gnawed on his.

"What's wrong?" she asked. "Isn't this what you wanted?"

He stared into her porcelain face. "Yes."

Her hands roved roughly, almost painfully up and down his back.

She backed away and released the top button on her blouse. Her shirt fell to the floor. Then her bra slipped off, and her voluptuous breasts fell free. Without the bra's support, her breasts sagged under gravity's pull.

She ripped open his shirt and sucked on his nipple. "Ouch!" Jake said.

She returned to his lips. Soft breasts squished against his bare chest. Jake was living his fantasy, but something was missing.

Her tongue made its way down his neck. She was trying to be erotic, licking his stomach, but there was no mystery in the hurried way she found his pants and undid the zipper.

She took his limp member in her mouth and sucked with a throbbing, pulsating pressure.

"Don't you like it?" she asked.

"This has never happened to me before." He didn't want to admit the full truth of that statement. Jake had never been naked with a woman. His nerves must have affected him. Why did his penis choose now to be unresponsive when he normally couldn't turn it off?

She pushed him onto the couch. "Sitting is better for the circulation."

She might as well have been sucking on his finger.

"Listen," Jake said. "You can stop."

She sucked with more vigor, humming with a fake enthusiasm Jake recognized from a hundred pornos.

"You can stop," he said again.

At last he stood, pushing her away. She grabbed his member violently and pulled him painfully toward her. He yanked her hand away and pulled up his pants.

"Maybe we could just watch some TV," he said.

"I can do better," she said, eyes pleading.

"I'd better go," Jake said. "I'm sorry. It's my fault. I'll call you tomorrow."

"You better."

It was too much for Jake, this happening all at once. He needed to take things slower. "We can have a proper date tomorrow," he said.

She gave him a goodbye kiss that could melt paint off the wall, but Jake felt nothing. He ran down the hall and out the main door.

The next morning Jake awoke relaxed and alert. He had slept late. He kicked off the sheet and looked down. His penis, normally the thing that woke him in the morning, remained limp and lifeless.

He shook it. "Wake up, little guy. It's alright. We're alone."

He got out his porno magazines and covered himself with lotion, a Saturday morning tradition. Back and forth he stroked the lifeless, hanging flesh.

"What's wrong with you?"

He dressed and took the trash out. The neighbor girl from downstairs sat on the outside step with her nose buried in a book. Her short hair was red today. It was different every time Jake saw her. Her pear shaped body was squeezed into torn jeans. A black sports bra showed through her white tank top.

"Hey, Jake," she said.

"Hey," he said. "Reading anything good?"

"No. I just had to get out of the apartment. Cable's out. Roommate's asleep. Bored." She looked Jake up and down. "There's something different about you, Jake."

He recognized the look. Perhaps this was what he needed, a test drive with someone who wasn't as important to him as Megan. "You want to watch some television at my place?" he asked.

"Sure."

Even with the windows open, the apartment still stank of rank magic. The piles of dirty laundry and molding dishes probably didn't help.

She circled the apartment. "Wow, Jake. You need a maid."

"Are you volunteering?" He couldn't believe his newfound

bravado.

"Yeah, right. I don't even clean our apartment."

She stopped in front of the bedroom and smiled. The magazines were still spread over the bed next to the lotion.

"You weren't bored, were you, Jake?"

"No. I was just—"

"I know what you were doing, Jake, but I'm here now." She pressed her young body against him, but he felt nothing. "What's the matter, Jake? You prefer your magazines?"

At last, he couldn't take it anymore. He pushed her away and out of the apartment.

She pounded at the door. "You can't get away with this, Jake! Fucking perv."

That night, Jake and Megan tried again to make love. Even on top of her, their naked bodies intertwined, his body wouldn't respond.

There could be no doubt. The ritual had done something to him. He could get any woman he wanted, but couldn't act on it.

He needed to summon up the demoness again, get the spell removed. He had spent more than he could afford gathering the ingredient the first time.

Megan lay beside him in the bed. Her fingers danced lightly on his bare chest. "Don't worry," she said. "This happens to guys. At least, I've heard that it does. It'll pass."

She looked at him as though she really cared.

"I might be able to fix it," Jake said, "but I need money."

She grinned. "I can get money."

She snuggled into his arms. Would she still care if the spell were reversed? A moment like this was worth impotence, but the magic was frustrating Megan and it frustrated Jake to watch her suffer. She needed a whole man. Jake prayed that man would be him.

Jake placed the flaming mojo in the center of the candles. The smell, after a week of cleanliness, made him want to vomit. Megan had taken a day off work to clean his apartment for him, which seemed out of character. Jake wondered how much of the Megan he had spent time with was really her, and how much was the magic.

He called the demon woman by name and waited.

After twenty minutes he called to her again. With tears in his eyes, he begged to have her gift removed.

His groin twitched, and his tears stopped. His member wiggled back and forth, struggling to be free.

Jake giggled and unzipped his pants.

He gasped. There on a bed of curly hair, instead of the familiar sight, rose the miniaturized, swiveling waist of the writhing demon woman. There was no distinction where his skin ended and hers began. Her shark-like mouth laughed silently as her breasts witnessed the horror on Jake's face.

Jake's breath came in quick, shallow gulps. Even with his eyes clenched, he could feel her undulating back and forth. He hated the demon, but he hated himself more. He had given himself to her.

His pain was even worse now that he knew what it was like to have someone care.

He rifled through the kitchen drawers. Ever since the apartment had been cleaned, he couldn't find anything. At last he found the meat cleaver. He raised it high into the air.

She actually looked frightened.

How much of himself was left? If he brought the blade down, he wouldn't be a man anymore.

He heard a door outside the apartment and thought of the neighbor girl— so young, so vivacious. Horror and self-hatred were replaced by animalistic need. The demon licked her lips. A week of suppressed urges hit Jake all at once.

Jake never saw Megan again. He had to leave town to keep himself away. If he had tried to say goodbye, he wouldn't have been able to stop himself from taking her. If he had tried to warn her, she wouldn't have been able to stay away from him.

None of them could ever stay away.

He couldn't bear the thought of seeing Megan killed like all the others, consumed by the devil in his pants.

HANDS THAT DO THE DEVIL'S WORK
BENJAMIN LANGLEY

Welcome, welcome, take a seat. How do you like the feel of that sofa? It's a Denelli Italia. I could have gone for something a little more expensive – I was tempted by the genuine alligator leather–but they say when you sit on a Denelli it's like you're sitting on a cloud. I can see it on your face; I'm not wrong, am I? Some say that's as close to heaven as you can get. What do you say? How does it feel? Can you put it into words?

Many can't. They sit there, and they tell me the luxury is indescribable. Heh. Indescribable.

Would you like a drink? I have a bottle of fifty-year-old Balvenie single malt–by all accounts, exquisite.

Hugo, bring our guest a glass of the Balvenie…

No, nothing for me.

Did you enjoy the scenery on your approach? The coastal path offers a great view over the cliffs and to the sea. If you're quiet for a second, and if you listen closely, you can hear the waves crashing against the rocks. It was that sound that brought me here, that's kept me here all these years.

Of course I miss the hubbub of the city, but I'm capable of working from home. Huh, I guess I have to. And I take it that's why you're here. You know my reputation–back in the day I was the guy that tore up contracts. If you wanted out of a bad deal, I was your man. I led many a client merrily through the loopholes and out the other side significantly better off than when they started. Whether that was a mismatched marriage or a bad business deal, I was the one that set people free.

With bigger wins came bigger contracts: multi-national organisations wanting out of their environmental obligations, clauses invoked to stop huge bonus pay-outs to front-of-house workers, revoking protection on areas of natural beauty.

No contract is entirely watertight, that's what I used to tell my clients. But these days I write the contracts. Maybe I could have used my talent in a more socially conscious way... if I'd have done that, I'd doubt I'd be here now. I certainly wouldn't have had the same reputation, and my reputation led Randolph Price to me, and without Randolph Price I never would have ended up in this house.

Let me tell you about Price. As soon as he entered my office, I could see the anxiety dripping from his brow, could hear it in the quiver of his voice, and as soon as he dropped the contract onto my desk, I knew I was dealing with something quite unlike I'd ever handled before.

The leaves of paper, oddly beige, did not sit together as one would expect, curling away from each other as if each page were disgusted by the words on the next.

"What is this?" I said, looking Price in the eyes. He'd made his appointment by phone, and had given me very few details about the deal he wanted out of. Naturally I did my research before our appointment. Price was the very epitome of privilege: privately educated at the very best schools, handed property when he turned twenty-four and sent out into the world armed with the security of a hatful of stocks and shares. All this was soon frittered away with a series of poor investments and business ventures steeped in failure. Having sold the property, he looked like he was going to be bankrupt by the time he was thirty, but then he turned it round. His luck on the stock market completely changed and he found a knack for buying low and selling high, and his software companies found success and huge profits with their every endeavour. But before me, Randolph Price, on the eve of his fortieth birthday, looked the very picture of a broken man.

In the images I'd seen online, Price looked a well-groomed gentleman, never a hair out of place and always immaculately dressed. In my office, he was unshaven, unwashed, unkempt. It was clear that the contents of the contract troubled him deeply.

"Whatever the problem is, Mr Price, I can help," I said, hoping to set him at ease. I disliked the thought of him shedding hair onto my carpet through his anxiety, and liked the idea of him sweating through his suit onto the Fritz Hansen Oxford premium office chair even less. The thought of skimming through the contract while he excreted onto my furniture was too unnerving, too distracting. If only he would give me a precis, I could begin to work my mind before I delved into the finer details of the wording of the contract.

Price stared only at the floor, muttering something incomprehensible.

"Okay, Mr Price, first, tell me what it is that you don't want to lose."

Price looked up. His eyes were bloodshot, livid with fear, and when he spoke it was in a voice that could barely carry the weight of words. "My hands." He held them out before me, trembling.

I glanced at the contract. Surely its terms did not dictate that he must pay the price with his hands, but I could not for the life of me understand what it could mean figuratively.

"Tell me, Mr Price, with whom did you come to such an agreement?" I asked.

He spoke in a whisper, and at first I thought he said "cushion," and I was ready to sling him out of my office. While he'd promised me millions if I could save him from the terms of his contract, I had no time for one as irrational as he. If only I had...

"I'm sorry?" I said.

He spoke louder. "With Gusion. A Duke from Hell." Price held his hands at face height. "He wants my hands."

I picked up the contract. It was all I could do to keep hold of it, for the coarse feel of the paper revolted me. It was some kind of pale leather, and the pages were stitched together with a thick brown fibre. I turned to the back page, each contact sending an unpleasant prickling sensation from my nerve endings all the way up my spine, but I persisted to see the signatories. There in crude dirty brown letters, the name Price had given me: Gusion.

Initially I thought this had to be either some kind of practical joke or that the man was deranged. It was one of those moments when I was truly lost for words, and believe me, you don't get all of this luxury in life if you if you can't talk a good game.

Price though, filled the silence for me, staring with intensity, his whole body shaking. "Ask him a question, and Gusion sees all. He controls forty-five legions of demons, and he tells all past, present, and future things."

I remembered my research–how close Price was to ruin. Was his sudden reversal in fortune as result of this bargain? "You signed a contract with a demon?" I asked.

He grimaced. "I was at rock-bottom! What else was I supposed to do? For ten years he has guided my every move, but the contract is shortly due to expire, and I must pay the price."

"And the price is your hands? Why your hands?"

"He says he needs more hands to do the devil's work." Price wept. "My hands!"

"Leave this with me, and I shall be in touch within twenty-four hours. Don't worry, Mr Price, I've yet to find a contract I can't find a way out of," I said, for at the time that was the truth.

I had a process: read from cover to cover, quickly at first to understand what has been promised. If necessary, I talk to any involved parties to confirm whether the promise of the contract has been delivered in full–those are the easiest outs– but in this case it was clear that Price was indeed given 'information on investments that would lead to significant profits'. In return for this, it stated, 'after a period of ten years I shall take both of your hands in their entirety.'

The contract was well-written, which was to be expected, for if there was any profession well represented in Hell, it was law. But it was only a matter of time before a drip of liberty dropped from the pages. I called Price, told him I had a way out, and that I would need to meet with him and this Duke from Hell to formalise the termination of the contract.

The next day, the eve of his fortieth birthday and the ten-year anniversary of the signing of the contract, Randolph Price arrived at my office. He had put on a new suit, one less drenched in sweat, and he'd shaved. "Are you sure this is going to work?" he said.

I urged him to sit. "Trust me." I said.

I see you've finished you drink? Would you like another? Or I have an exquisite port. The 1985 Smith Woodhouse Vintage… Hugo, another drink for our guest.

Once Price was seated, I asked him to summon Gusion. Before my very eyes, in the corner of my room, a rectangular shape materialised. It started with a glow, before the lick of flames formed the shape of a door. As it opened, a figure, smaller than an average man, emerged. When he got down on all fours and started to move towards us, I realised that this must indeed be Gusion, for once more I had done my research, and discovered his name in an ancient text, *The Lesser Key of Solomon*. The information there corresponded with what Price had revealed, and also stated that he took the form of the baboon which I saw before me.

Once he was close I could see the hideous effect of a lifetime among the flames of Hell, for his tail was blackened and singed and on one side of his proboscis was the scar of a burn, swirling the flesh, leaving it smooth in some places, wrinkled in others, casting one side of his face in a permanent sneer.

He spoke in a high voice, but one steeped in authority. "It is time, Price, to pay for your decade of fortune. Come." With a swing of his arm, he ushered us to follow him, and returned through that magical entrance.

Through the open door, the fires of Hell glowed and the screams of the damned echoed, and yet I stood with confidence, contract in hand, ready to go through and argue the logic of my case. As soon as we were on the other side, the door disappeared, not so much as in a puff of smoke, but in a cloud of it, and while I trusted my process, I felt fear gnawing at my innards.

The room beyond the door resembled a courtroom, albeit one decimated by fire and decorated with glistening bone. The gallery was filled with vile, red-skinned beings, perhaps once human, or denizens borne of Hell itself. Their demented wails filled the room as we followed Gusion, who positioned himself on the left, so, naturally, I led Price to the other side. Through the open doors at the back of the chamber, accompanied by the sound of trumpets wielded by bedraggled creatures, charred flesh flaking from their bones, entered a winged creature, almost angelic in form, but bearing every sign of evil epitomised.

Gusion leant forward. "You have sought the representation of an expert, as is your right, Price. As is mine, I call upon Lucifer, Lord of the Netherworld, master of all demons, to preside over court. Now, let this so-called expert of yours speak."

I nodded towards Lucifer, and I have to admit at this point I felt more than a little out of my depth. The corners of his mouth turned up into a sinister smile, and he allowed his blackened wings to stretch out behind him to reveal the extent to which the bones were broken. His skin radiated a glow as if he revelled in the pain and the memory of the fall it evoked. But if there is one thing that is true of demons, even the lord of all demons, it is that while they are deceptive and manipulative, they are true to their word and would never break the terms of a contract. I had to have faith in the words on the page and my ability to interpret them truthfully.

"I have read the contract…" I paused for a moment, not quite knowing which form of address to use before settling upon something appropriate given his status, "your Highness. And indeed, it does state that Gusion may take the hands of my client."

The baboon demon showed his teeth with a cruel smile, and I turned slightly to catch Price's reaction, witnessing the last of the colour drain from his face.

"I invite you to take, as it states, both hands in their entirety," I said, gesturing towards Price.

Lucifer snapped his fingers, and a cleaver materialised on the desk in front of Gusion.

Upon seeing it, Price tucked his arms behind his back.

I continued. "I must warn you, however, that the terms of this contract are very clear. You must take both hands... but you may not take so much as a slither of the wrist. Should you take so much as a thread of tendon or the tendon sheaths belonging to the wrist, or spill so much as a drop of fluid from the bursae then you will be in forfeit of the contract, and should you decide to be cautious in your approach, and leave so much as a hint of the hand on the wrist, you will also be in forfeit of the contract, for it states you must take both hands in their entirety. Now go ahead. Chop away."

Price continued to hold his hands behind his back, his face a picture of abject terror.

I turned to him. "Trust me," I said, and slowly he withdrew his hands and placed them on the desk.

Gusion took hold of the cleaver. Moving on three limbs, and wielding the weapon above his head, he hurried to our table and carefully examined Price's trembling hands.

As Gusion continued his study, the demonic crowd looked on, thirsty for bloodshed, their palpable excitement audible through the single unified heartbeat that signalled the passing seconds.

After scrutinising Price's hands from every possible angle, Gusion gave out a yelp of frustration and walked away, shaking his head. "Lucifer," he said, "I fear I already know your answer. Is it possible?"

The king of demons shook his head.

"Then I concede. You know it is impossible to remove the hands without some kind of damage to aspects of the wrist. Upon his death, when he is only bone, I shall take what is owed to me."

"Then we are agreed that my client is free to go," I said.

Lucifer raised a finger. "Gusion," he said, "it is correct that you know all future things, is that true?"

"In so far as when I am asked a question, I can see the answer, even if it lies at some distant time."

"Then before we let our friend, the lawyer, go, I have a question for you."

Gusion smiled a cruel smile, revealing his sharp canines. "Go ahead."

"Will our friend, the master of contracts here, return to us one day?"

Gusion looked directly at me, and laughed, and soon his laugh was echoed by that of Lucifer, followed by the cruel laughs of the demon trumpeters and the members of the galley.

The door through which we'd arrived re-appeared, still edged with flame and I couldn't get through it quick enough, covering my ears as Price followed.

On the other side, back in my office, I could share none of his joy. It was clear to see the relief on his face, but I was deaf to his words, the laughter of demons still ringing in my ears, laughter that continued wherever I went, following me both indoors and out, so that I couldn't work, but at night it was always worse, echoing around my head, denying me sleep, torturing me.

I had to get away. I had to find solace somewhere. It was Price that put me onto this place, part of his portfolio of properties, and with what he'd paid me, I had more than enough to buy this house, right by the sea, where the sound of the waves drowned out the sound of the laughter.

When I came here, I found peace. Huh! It was almost as if they weren't laughing anymore, and that's when I made the fatal mistake. I signed the contract without reading every single word. I assumed it was like every other property contract I'd signed, and in truth it was, with the exception of a couple of clauses.

As I said, when in the house, I was deaf to the laughter of

demons, and as such, I was keen to move in as early as possible, but on that first night, as I climbed into my bed–a six-thousand spring Majesty, and my head hit the luxury Hungarian goose-down pillows, the laughter echoed once more, followed by the words, "You're mine." And when the laughter stopped, I couldn't feel the softness of the pillow, or the fine thread of the sheets. I climbed out, and as I did so a gust of wind (from where I do not know, for the windows were closed) blew something from the dresser. It was the contract. It had fallen open on the thirteenth page, a clause circled in red ink:

While occupying the house, the purchaser will be unable to experience the sensation of taste or of touch, and upon leaving the house, or death, the purchaser will immediately become the property of Lucifer.

So as you sit in my luxurious chair, I urge you to enjoy the texture of the fabric, the way that it hugs your figure. If you have words that can describe that simple pleasure, please share them. And drink my drink and a simple word to share your experience will be greatly appreciated, for I can experience none of it. It brings me such misery, that at times I am tempted to end it all, only I know he awaits me.

And that's not all, for there was another clause inserted into the contract, one of which I'm sure you're aware, the one which brings you to me today.

While living in the premises, the occupier must carry out work on behalf of Lucifer or his legion.

So I built my reputation as the man who gets others out of dodgy contracts. I once believed that no contract was water-tight. Now here I am. It's my hands that do the devil's work, writing contracts for the likes of you, contracts that allow you to prey on the weak and needy, harvest their limbs and their organs once you've rendered your services, contracts that you and I know there's no getting out of.

If I have nothing else, I still have my professional pride, so what do you need?

PROM QUEEN
JULIA C. LEWIS

Thick fog swirled around the dim bedroom, almost completely obscuring the candles standing on the scratched-up hardwood floor. The flames flickered helplessly as an icy cold wind swished by them. Dozens of black candles were arranged in a circle around a cloaked shape sitting on her knees in the middle of a painted pentagram. The red color of the paint glistened in the candlelight, and the figure spoke out once more.

"Oh, come to me, Dark Lord. Bless me with your presence and I shall offer you my soul." The teenage girl closed her eyes and lowered her torso to the floor in a devoted bow.

The wind became stronger as she finished her ritual, and a loud booming noise soon joined the commotion within the room. As the girl sat up and opened her eyes, she saw a hulking shape standing near the door to her bedroom. The form was massive, about seven feet tall, and had to stand slightly hunched over to avoid colliding with the ceiling. Two twisted horns topped his head, and instead of feet he had goat-like hooves. But that wasn't what the young girl was staring at, no; she was way more fascinated with the rock-solid six pack the demon seemed to sport.

As if annoyed by her incessant staring, the demon spoke out with a bellow, "Umm…so… You called?"

Startled by the loud voice, the girl crawled backwards and pulled her knees to her chest. Her mind had gone blank at the sight of him, and she couldn't utter a single word.

"So, listen. I was in the middle of something, and you're gonna need to get it together and tell me what you want." The demon glanced down at his nonexistent watch and tapped it with his enormous black claw.

The girl cleared her throat and whispered, "I-I need you to take care of someone for me. Her name is Jenna, and I want her dead."

"Dead? Do I look like the Grim Reaper to you? Girl, you got the wrong man for the job." He crossed his arms over his broad chest, running his enormous tongue over his fangs.

"No, wait! My name is Lisa and my friend Mindy said you can help me! She told me to call on Lucifer himself and offer him my soul in exchange..." She looked at him pleadingly.

"Alright, alright. I can't say no to a delicious soul. *But* don't go running around telling everyone about this. I don't want my reputation ruined. Deal?"

"D-Deal."

"I will *get rid* of this Jenna for you, and in exchange you will hand over your soul at the time of your demise. There are no take backs and once you agree, there's no turning back. Before you agree, though, tell me *why* you want her dead so badly."

The girl took a deep breath. "It all started last summer, when I went to prom with Bryce Greene from our high school. He is the hottest guy at school, and, at first, I was really confused as to why he was into me. As you can see, I'm not the prettiest girl, and, well, boys usually agree with that. So, when he came to me right before senior prom and asked me to go with him, I thought he was messing with me.

"I had secretly hoped for that moment ever since Bryce came to our school back in 9th grade. You can't imagine how loud I was screaming internally when he approached me with his beautiful green eyes. They twinkle in the fluorescent lighting of the hallway, and well....

"Anyways, my friend Elena was over the moon and couldn't quit talking about what this would mean for me. Going out with a popular guy was like the holy grail and I had somehow snatched him up. I had of course told him that yes, I would go with him, but deep down I felt like something wasn't right. I wasn't sure if he had lost a bet or someone was daring him to hang out with me, but I couldn't say no. I had to believe he truly was interested in me.

"Around the same time Bryce had asked me out, this super popular girl named Jenna started sprouting rumors about me all over school. She told everyone how easy I was and that I had been to the football team's locker room on more than one occasion. Of course, I was way too scared to tell her off, so I let her say whatever she wanted about me, even if it obviously wasn't true. She was probably just jealous, even though I had no idea what of.

"A few days before the prom, I asked my mom and dad for some money for a new dress. I had seen this gorgeous blue floral one in the shop the day before, and I knew it was expensive, but they had to realize how important this was. When I told them how much money I needed, they looked at each other and then burst out laughing. I stormed off crying to my room and slammed the door.

"So, I did the only thing I could think of and used the book my friend Mindy had given me to summon Astaroth, the demon of—"

"Hold on, hold on right there! You already summoned a demon before? And this demon was Astaroth out of all people? The freakin' demon of vanity. So, what did you offer him?" Lucifer sighed and rolled his eyes.

"Oh, that. Yeah, he was actually super easy to make an offering to. All he wanted was my mom's jewelry."

"Does your mom know that?" He looked at her in mock concern.

"She thinks we had a break-in. Could I finish my story now?" the girl asked questioningly.

"Okay, but make it quick. I got things to do."

"After I summoned Astaroth and he gave me this fiery red dress, I was overjoyed. It looked like it came from some high-end designer that only the richest celebrities would own. To be honest, the fabric did put me off a bit at first, especially since it felt like stiff leather, but then again, I wasn't going to resummon the demon and tell him I didn't like it. He might actually kill me for that, and who cares if it had a weird little owl etched onto the back that looked almost identical to my cousin Rose's tattoo? I was sure it was all a coincidence, probably demon magic or whatever you guys do in hell.

"Anyhow, I could barely believe how amazing I looked in it, and I was hyped for prom. I swear the dress gave me curves I'd never had before. The days went by super slowly and I had a hard time concentrating at school. I flunked a math test for the first time in my life and was starting to get really concerned about getting grounded right before prom. Luckily, my parents never saw the graded test, because, you know... I 'lost' it.

"On the night of the prom, Bryce picked me up in a black limo and he was actually speechless when he was me in my dress. He kept smiling his handsome smile at me, and put his arm around me on the drive. I knew then that it had all been worth it. Once we got to the gym where the dance was being held, I walked inside with the most confidence I had ever had in my entire life. I felt radiant.

"Upon our entrance, I could have sworn everyone stopped what they were doing and stared at the two of us. It was exactly like in the movies. We had an amazing night dancing and talking until—"

"Is this story going somewhere?" Lucifer had by now sat on the girl's dresser, careful not to splinter the wood.

Putting her hands to her face in frustration, Lisa said, "Dude! Let me finish! A little while later, they announced the prom king and queen, and to no surprise it was Bryce and me. We made our way up on stage, everyone cheering in the background, when he winked at me. It almost melted my heart. So, there I was, about to receive my crown, when a bucket of pig's—"

"Stop... now you're just retelling a famous horror book."

"Okay, fine. I'm sorry, I just wanted it to be really dramatic." Lisa pouted at Lucifer. "What really happened was, they crowned me prom queen and Bryce leaned in for a kiss right there on the stage, when a used tampon hit me straight in the face.

"Bryce looked at me in disgust, and I was frozen in place,

not knowing how to react. I'm pretty sure it wasn't actually used, most likely just painted with a red sharpie, but at that moment it seemed real enough. Everyone was laughing and pointing at me. I wanted to vanish right there and then. I had never felt as humiliated in my entire life, and that bitch Jenna was laughing the loudest.

"I finally snapped out of my stupor, and ran from the stage. On the way to the girls' bathroom, I saw Jenna and her army of bitches standing in the hallway snickering to themselves. And that's why I called on you." The girl eyed the Dark Lord expectantly.

"Okay, so let me get this straight. You summoned me, the all-powerful Lucifer, to drag a girl to hell for throwing a maybe/maybe not used tampon at you? Are you crazy?"

"It was humiliating, and Bryce just started ghosting me after that. I had to call my dad to pick me up from prom. He was so mad and kept going on and on about how selfish I was being. Telling me I should have stayed home and helped look for my cousin Rose, who had apparently not come home in a few days," the girl clicked her tongue in annoyance. "Worst thing is, the next week Bryce was standing in the hall at school with his arm around Jenna. He was supposed to be mine. MINE!" The girl balled her fists in fury.

"I get it. You're mad. So, let's talk punishment, then. I got an array of torture devices down there. I got Iron Maidens, The Rack, some Judas Cradles, oh! And my favorite: good old crucifixion!"

The girl bit her index finger and said, "I don't care. Just something that hurts."

"Sign this blood bound contract and, in exchange for your soul, I will drag Jenna to Hell." The demon suddenly held a paper contract in his hands and handed the girl a fancy golden pen and a small dagger. Without hesitation, she sliced her palm and let her blood flow freely onto the floor beneath her. Dipping the pen into the maroon liquid, she signed her name, and Lucifer instructed her to close her eyes and he would show her a vision of him fulfilling the deed. With great anticipation, the girl sat on her bed and closed her eyes.

The Dark Lord appeared within a teenager's bedroom adorned with boy band posters and big stuffed bears sitting on a bench in the corner. Lisa could only guess that this was Jenna's bedroom, as she had never even been close to being invited to the popular girl's house. Jenna was peacefully sleeping in her bed when Lucifer stomped towards her and yanked her pink comforter away from her.

The girl responded with a terrified scream and tried to shuffle away from the demonic figure. To her dismay, Lucifer was a lot faster than her and he grabbed her by the wrist and brought her to a standing position. Even though Lisa hated Jenna with all her might, the snapping of her delicate wrist bones in the giant's hands still made her cringe. Next, the demon mumbled some words and a fiery hole opened on the bedroom floor. Within seconds both the Dark Lord and Jenna were gone.

Back in her own bedroom, Lisa smiled to herself.

Some sixty years later...

Lisa, now an old woman near death, lay in her hospital bed, living out her final days in this mortal realm. She looked over and smiled weakly at the man hunched over on a chair next to her. Her husband Bryce had been her rock for her entire life and they had spent many happy years together. With tears forming in her eyes, she mouthed, *I love you.*

When she woke next, clinging to life by a mere thread, a familiar bulking form was standing at the foot of her bed. Lucifer held out his hand and beckoned her to join him.

"The time has come. You swore your soul to me and I've come to collect."

The frail old woman struggled to get up, but Lucifer aided her. He was a demon hungry for souls, after all.

He looked down at his newest liege and smiled. "Oh, before I forget. I wanted to thank you for letting me have Jenna all those years ago. She has proven herself to have quite the talent for torturing souls herself. In fact, she joined my hellish team as head torturer over in the women's ward just a few months ago. She said she's eager to see you."

As the fiery hole opened in the hospital floor, the Dark Lord clutched a crying and screaming Lisa to his six-pack abs.

IN THE DETAIL
LIAM A SPINAGE

Letitia stood alone on the balcony, glass in hand, looking out over the night sky. Far below her was the swirling fog of city lights: neon signs, headlamps, streetlights. Mere pinpricks at that distance, but they melded together in a medley of memories. There had been times when she had been behind one of those lights, like so many other people in the city, not detached from it there in the penthouse. She swirled the champagne in the flute, sending bubbles scattering like flies. The sweet glass of victory twinkled in the suffused glow of the apartment lighting and the candle she had precariously balanced on the balcony table next to her, sputtering in the breeze but remaining defiant. She felt a lot of empathy for that candle. A tiny, exhaustible flicker of passion against a sky of brooding, monotonous darkness.

Still lost in thought, she took a tentative sip, relishing the cool feeling as it trickled down her throat. The rest of the bottle sat on the table next to the candle, still chilling in the ice bucket. She would save that for later. There were reasons to celebrate that night, but the past five years had installed within her a certain degree of caution. Not for the first time, but maybe - just maybe - for the last, she reflected on that momentous decision five years ago which had fundamentally changed her life.

The door buzzer sounded from deep within the apartment. She paused for a moment, but the buzzer did not. She usually had someone to deal with these interruptions, but she had dismissed her staff for the evening so that she would not be disturbed. Except by him, obviously, although she hadn't thought he would approach in such a mundane way. A puff of smoke, maybe, a whiff of sulphur, a flash of bright flame. But no, he was about to enter in the same way that everyone else did.

She reached towards the white marble table and delicately deposited her glass there. Then she began to make her way back through her spacious lodgings. A four-poster bed with white satin drapes and twinkling dimmed fairy lights for that otherworldly feel. A spotless lounge, floored in white polished marble and a single small but perfectly placed rug. Busts of Medea, Circe and Ariadne sourced from the finest auction houses in the city and the world beyond. An entry room with a spacious cloakroom to one side, hidden behind black velvet curtains. Effortlessly, she raised a manicured finger and released the latch. As the handle turned, she paced back into the lounge and struck a pose on the scarlet chaise longue opposite the overstuffed armchair. That was the single item of furniture which stuck out in her otherwise immaculately appointed paradise, and it was there for a reason. It was the only memory she allowed herself from her former life. Until then.

She could hear his footsteps and the click of his cane approaching. *Something wicked this way comes.* A moment of rustling where he had clearly divested himself of an outer garment in the allotted place. A rushing intake of breath as he surveyed the sheer majesty of what he had helped her to afford. As he approached, Letitia faltered for a moment. His very presence drew her back to that time when they had first met, when the power difference between them had been a gulf between worlds. The sheer malignancy of that shadow, even when dressed in human form, drew her in like a moth to a flame. For the first time, she began to wonder whether the strategy she had devised would work. She shivered, trembled even, at every footstep until she glimpsed herself momentarily in the mirror and saw her younger self, high on life, drunk on her own confidence, about to make what could easily be the biggest and most dangerous mistake of her life. She barely recognised that young girl in herself after all this time. She was different now. Not just richer, but more mature, more experienced. Her inner confidence grew, and she regained her composure just as he spoke to her.

"Good evening. I see you were expecting me." His voice, low but sonorous, more than a hint of mischief, the same as it had been five years ago.

Finally, she turned to meet his face. Though she was sure it was just the same after all this time, the balance between them had shifted slightly. That face had haunted and taunted her over the years, reflected in dozens of shop windows, revolving doors, cocktail glasses, champagne flutes. Was it just her imagination or had he been with her every step of the way, looking, laughing, crowing, waiting? Just how much of her life did he know?

The face was still long and lean. In the light of the bar where they had first met, it had been sweaty, sallow even, yet still handsome. That's what had first attracted her to him. His lashes, his moustaches. There were few well-groomed and well-dressed individuals in that dive. She had instantly wanted to know his story. He, in turn, had instantly wanted to know hers. The night had passed slowly, exchanges between them became more friendly, more fervent. Then, as she gazed into his hypnotising grey eyes, he had made her an offer she couldn't refuse.

"Hello, you old devil. Has it really been five years?"

His face was different now, she realised. The line of his lips which had once been so willing to laugh now formed a sneer, giving way as he spoke to betray the immense hunger behind those perfect white teeth. She instinctively gulped, trying not to show it. If she showed fear now, all would be lost.

"It has. As you well know. And now I arrive at the appointed hour to collect what is due. I see that you have been enjoying your gift." He extended an arm sleeved in a dark suit - charcoal grey, she thought in the dim light, with a flash of bright red lining - as a sweep around the penthouse.

"I have not forgotten. Please, sit." She gestured at the cracked leather of the armchair. He bowed slightly, mockingly, and did so.

"I'm here to collect, waitress."

She laughed, deep and rich and long. He joined in.

"It's been a long time since I've been that. But still, I have a memory of that night when we first met, see? You're sitting on it. That's the armchair from the staff break room where you sat as I poured out my hopes and fears and you offered me the world on a plate. A simple transaction, really." Was it her imagination or did he actually begin to look uncomfortable? Had he perhaps an inkling of what was about to happen?

"I recall it well, waitress."

Well. To be addressed in that manner a second time was simply rude. Not that she considered the devil above petty manipulation, far from it. He was trying to put her off-kilter. Playing with his food before he devoured her utterly.

"Do you also recall..." she tailed off, lost for a moment in the handsomeness of his lean face, those hungry eyes, that perfect chin. "Do you recall what it was I asked of you?"

"I do, but I don't need to. It's all here." From the interior of his suit jacket, he withdrew a single piece of paper and let it unfurl, first from his wrist to the arm of the chair and then across the floor, stopping finally at the outline of the rug. "Second thoughts, waitress? It's a little too late for that. Five years too late, I should say. Don't be coy. You accepted the gift, now accept the consequences." He leaned forward in a gesture of quiet menace clearly honed by what she imagined was millennia of practice. Behind him on the wall, his shadow loomed large even while he remained seated. Though her rooms were lit with the brightest lamps, the shadow he cast now - and the shadow he had cast over her life for the last five years - threatened to drown her in darkness.

"Yes. Success. That's what I traded my soul for. Success in my chosen occupation. And that has worked out very well for me, very well indeed, I must agree. I have the world at my feet." She stood quietly, in one lithe movement, her pearls swaying slowly at her alabaster throat.

"There must be a particular thirst for cocktails that I was

unaware of at the time. Who would have thought!"

She moved in stockinged feet to the scroll now fully unfurled across the room and removed an elegant pair of glasses from a case in her purse. He seemed to anticipate this move.

"They always think there's something in the contract that can get them out." This was barely perceptible to Letitia, almost a mutter, but it echoed nevertheless around the empty space between them and hung, lingering in the air with a faint whiff of threat and sulphur. He spoke it as if an aside to a hidden third party. Or perhaps to himself, a mote of contempt for his victims which he had only vocalised so that she could feel the cruel, casual mockery in his voice.

"Oh, I'm sure many have tried!" She attempted a laugh, but it came out a little hoarse, a little stilted. He was beginning to sense her fear. "It's quite clear, though. You're right." She knelt before the lengthy contract and squinted briefly at the small print before beginning to read the first line. "I, Letitia Maria de Santis do, on this day of November 27th 1981, at the hour of 3 AM, enter into this agreement whereby I will be granted unparalleled success in my chosen profession for five years in return for which at the appointed hour five years from now I will relinquish my soul to the devil in payment," She shot a glance across at him over the rim of her glasses delicately balanced on the bridge of her nose. On the mantle, perched between two alabaster busts, a golden clock ticked slowly, irrevocably, towards that very hour.

"So?" He rubbed his hands together in glee. "What are we waiting for?"

"It's the small print that interests me."

"Oh?" He appeared unperturbed. "Most people don't even give that a second glance. I mean, what's a few extra words in comparison to five years of fame and riches?"

"Is it always five years?" The question seemed to shock him a little and he tilted his head a little, his brows raised quizzically.

"It is traditional, yes. Just enough rope for people to hang themselves with, you see. Oh, I know…" here he brushed off a little yellow dust from his shoulder as easily as he brushed off her question, "I know that fifteen minutes of fame was all the rage some while back, but what we savour is the anticipation of doom that a contract end represents. Why, you wouldn't believe the lengths some people go to trying to get out of the deal. Or maybe you would?" At that last line, the inflection in his voice changed slightly, becoming more contemplative. Then he laughed again, and the moment was lost. "You're not trying to negotiate an extension, are you? Oh, how simply delightful. It won't work, I'm afraid."

"And yet there is nothing here in any of the subclauses which necessarily precludes such an arrangement. I thought it at least worth a try."

"Sorry." He was not sorry. He was not an entity for which remorse, repentance or forgiveness could even exist. The word was a mere formality, an amuse-bouche to whet his appetite before his lean form sprang forward, pouncing voraciously on his trapped prey. "But when your number's up…"

"Yes, I understand". She got back to her feet and walked over to a cabinet on the far side of the room, flinging open the doors. "Still, it seems that at least I can offer you a drink while you're here?" The chair creaked as he turned it around slightly, arching his back to take in the full display of bottles available. There must have been over a hundred there, all manner of shapes and sizes, antique bottles covered in dust, cut glass carafes full of unknown concoctions, shiny new bottles of the most expensive spirits affordable on Earth.

"I will take one cocktail of your choosing, to humour you. After all, when you've been instrumental in making the career of the finest cocktail waitress in the world, it's a bonus to see what you have helped achieve. And then…you know what awaits."

As his gaze lingered, she felt him probing her mind. In that moment she finally knew her intended fate. Before her formed vistas of literal hellscapes – vast vats of blood and excrement in which wallowed the unfortunate, jagged cliffs screaming with the howls of chained prisoners, unending lakes of lava rippling as victims were thrown in over and over and over...

She steeled herself. It took all her strength; reserves of will began to wither within her. This would be her last chance.

"Very well. Allow me." Letitia busied herself for some moments, unstopping some bottles and inspecting the contents. Finally, she began pouring small measures into a cocktail shaker, reached into the cabinet and extracted two highball glasses. He seemed content to watch her in those silent moments, savouring the last hours of her life before he claimed it for eternity.

Turning her back on him - especially at such a critical juncture - might have been perceived as a power move. Certainly, Letitia could feel her power growing, though her hands still shook slightly as she uncorked a large bottle of fortified wine. Perhaps, just perhaps, this might actually work. Hiding her fear, she nevertheless wanted to know how he saw her at that moment. Was she still prey? Or, just maybe, boon companion? Dare she even imagine...adversary?

She could see him out of the corner of her eye, just about, but more keenly in the many reflective surfaces of the bottles arrayed before her. His lean figure, at ease in the armchair, his eager face watching her back, reflected and distorted by the different folds and twists in the antique bottles which lined the cabinet. His visage tinted blue here, green there from the contents of those bottles, elongated almost beyond recognition by the cut of the crystal decanters, fractured into multiple facades by the refraction of the light through the water, each proffering a different promise. But in each of them, clear as anything, were the glint of those grey, uncompromising, all-seeing eyes.

Finally, her task complete, she added an olive and a twist to each then made her way back to the chaise longue. Leaning over, she proffered him one of the glasses with a final flourishing swirl. The clear liquid sprang into life as hues of red and yellow began swirling around each other as if in mutual pursuit.

"Very clever!" He raised the glass to his ruby lips, taking in the heady aroma. Letitia mirrored the procedure.

"To us! Success at a price."

"To us!"

He took his first swallow of whatever deliciousness she had prepared. Letitia herself hesitated for a moment before she swallowed, waiting to see his reaction.

He began spluttering almost immediately, the liquid spraying from his mouth as he started to cough. Letitia looked over knowingly.

"What have you done? That was awful! Probably the worst thing I've ever tasted!" When he had recovered a little of his form, he reached into his jacket for a slate-grey silk handkerchief which, she noted, was even monogrammed with a little red 'L' in the corner. He held it to his lips, still occasionally retching, and wiped the spittle from his chin.

"I never was any good at making cocktails."

"What? I made you the best in the world! What have you done with that? How have you got all this wealth from so little talent?"

"I direct you again to the terms of our contract."

"I... What? You wanted to be the best at your chosen profession. What happened?"

"Correct. But that chosen profession wasn't making cocktails. I was only doing that to make ends meet during my studies. My chosen profession was contract law." She sipped at her own cocktail, unstirred, and looked back at him with an expression that was half-grimace, half-grin. "I do apologise if that happens to be a matter of confusion for you. The way the contract is worded wasn't specific about that, you see." She leaned forward conspiratorially, confident in her approach now. "But we can change that, you and I."

He could feel the power between them shifting slightly. He didn't like it.

"I'm quite sure I don't know what you mean."

"I mean that it's still possible for me to negotiate an extension. Now, you, as the party of the first part…"

"Wait, wait." He seemed to need time to think. Letitia thought this was amusing and her mouth betrayed the tiniest of smirks. But it wasn't over yet. Even as the balance between them began to tip in her favour, she couldn't afford to let it show fully. Still, she enjoyed watching him squirm as she swilled the contents of her glass. When she saw her own reflection in that glass, and his too, hovering on the edge, she was struck at the similarity between them. She looked up.

"Why wait? By accident, it seems that you have created the finest contract lawyer on earth. That's what has brought me all this fame, all these lovely curios, this wonderful penthouse apartment. You thought I got all this from inventing some new drink? Please. If I understand correctly - and here the print is quite clear - when I go with you then all this is over. All the gifts offered, this keen mind, this knowledge, are lost to me and you both. It's also clear that despite all rumour to the contrary, hell really does not have all the best lawyers. There are clauses here that are so ridiculously archaic as to be meaningless. Surely you would appreciate my insights into it before you take your prize back with you for an infinity of torture?"

As pitches go, she thought she'd nailed it. He seemed to agree, but then a wry smile took over his face again. "What you suggest should take no more than five hours, let alone five more years. Nevertheless, I concur. Fix me something that's actually palatable and let us both take a look at the fine print together. Maybe you really can teach this old dog some new tricks."

Three hours later, they looked up from a second contract, with even more confounding legalese and clauses than the devil could hope for. Vials of red and black ink lay strewn across the cold marble of the floor and the teak writing desk; a feather had escaped from a quill and was slowly meandering across the floor toward the balcony in a breeze-borne bid for freedom.

"Well." He stood straight and tall. "That is certainly an improvement. I cannot thank you enough."

Letitia raised a single perfectly plucked eyebrow. He laughed. "A mere figure of speech, something I am certain never to write down." He sobered again and extended a long bony hand toward her. "Now, come. You are done with this world."

"Oh, I don't think so." Letitia drained a tiny cup heavy with caffeine stains. She also stood, stretching as she did so. For the first time, she looked him in the eye and did not blink. Then she picked up her contract again and slowly crossed the space between them, her stockinged feet silent on the marble floor. "The devil may be in the detail, but this line of the contract is just heavenly." She pursed her lips to proffer a kiss into the air. "*In return for which, at the appointed hour.* I'm afraid to break it to you, but that appointed hour has come and gone." Her eyes flicked briefly back to the clock on the mantle.

Letitia handed him the contract which he started at, dumbfounded, as she moved lithely across the room, stopping in front of her bedroom door. "It is now eight in the morning." With that, she threw open the door with a flourish, flooding the room with light from the balcony beyond. "The sun has risen while you made work for my idle hands. All those extra clauses. Dear me. I'll have to leave you now." She squinted through the door to her bedroom and the balcony where the sun had risen magnificently. "I have an appointment with another morning star. I'm sure you can find your own way out."

Leaving the devil howling in frustrated rage, Letitia walked out into the light and poured herself another glass of champagne. She never had liked cocktails.

SANTA'S WORKSHOP
MICHELLE CRISTIANI

Palms don't sweat in Hell, but Sadie remembered what it had felt like. Her first year Helliversary was coming up. And after that, she'd be bottom of the heap, fair game to anyone. Maybe there was no sweat here, but there definitely was pain. She didn't want to think about what she'd endure. She'd seen it this year. The torture wouldn't end.

Why was she even here? Turns out, requirements for Heaven were as strict as the fanatics thought. It was, though, *eventually* attainable to anyone - making all Hell-dwellers just prisoners angling for parole. Sadie took a deep breath and recited again her mantra: "Hell is just Purgatory. Hell is just Purgatory." She wouldn't be here forever. Even if it seemed like it.

Even now, in death, Sadie still had the habit of playing with her blonde waves. It was a subconscious flirtation, like a beacon to all the humans (and now, demons). They came close enough so she could have felt their breath if they were breathing. They knew better than to touch. But she felt marked all the same.

She played with her hair, paced on, and recited again. "Hell is just Purgatory." Not forever. It was almost better to think about her life and death. And they had been horrible, too.

Sadie was a textbook sad song: drunken stepfather beat drunken mother while in drunken rages. The house was small and the fridge was always empty. She spent as little time there as she could, running with a crowd who always let her crash. There was only one thing Sadie loved in life, that made it worth living: not school, not clothes, not music. Drugs? Drugs were both dangerous and predictable. Sadie didn't touch drugs, not even a sip of beer. They led to ruin and she refused to be ruined. No, only one vice kept her going.

Sex. Sadie lived for sex.

What did that make her? She knew all the names. Didn't matter that she genuinely liked it, more than the boys did. She had her blonde and her natural curves and she was everybody's dream. Everybody's. And if she wasn't, she learned how to be.

On Sadie's 21st birthday she decided she was meant for sex work. Sure, she enjoyed sex, but could also be getting paid for what she hadn't yet explored. Now of age, she was ready for a new life. Manny drove her to the bus station - well, he was *supposed* to - but he'd been drinking, and she wanted to get out of there so much that she took the risk of riding with him anyway, and lost. She died that night, at twenty-one and a day. Died because of drugs. They killed her in the end despite all her efforts.

And there, contact with anyone was forbidden for six more days. On the seventh day, she wouldn't be safe, and the only sex she'd be having would be the non-consensual kind.

Good news at least, if there was any: Sadie wouldn't age anymore. All she had was her youthful body and what she could do with it. Granted, it would be all the more tempting to torturers here; but she wouldn't have to watch her body lose the only thing she was proud of. She was, in a sense, preserved. What a twisted, cruel way to avoid sagging skin and waning vitality. Drugs got her, but aging hadn't.

Avoiding her greatest fear - growing old - was ironic comfort. But Sadie was also claustrophobic. Maybe it seemed open here, and maybe it was in a sense endless. But despite the physical expanse, Sadie was literally stuck there. It wasn't about small spaces; it was about being trapped. Lungs didn't breathe in Hell, either, but Sadie could practically feel herself hyperventilate when she thought about herself there, for more time than her human brain could count, with no exit anywhere. She kept moving, watching bodily torture that should have been boring by now. No one ever seemed desensitized to it;

maybe souls were programmed that way. There was no escape. She wished more than ever she could take deep breaths, and close her eyes and ears. No corners to retreat to, anyway. She tried to walk without looking.

Didn't matter who she bumped into; she'd bounce, for now, off-limits. But people circled constantly, eyeing her ticking clock. She needed a way out. She wasn't ready for Heaven, and Heaven wasn't ready for her. There was another option - a long shot, but she had to do it.

She had to interview at Santa's workshop.

Sadie had literally no skills - well, other than the one. And Santa - all of them really - had their pick of countless beauties. Cleopatra was here, for fuck's sake. Sadie may have been special in her small town and small tank tops, but she wasn't special here. She squared her shoulders, and wished again she could take in breath, so that she could sigh. Her novelty, maybe, could be her selling point. Maybe she could work her way out of here before becoming someone's unwilling toy.

As Sadie expected, the line was very long, but it was moving quickly, which unnerved her. Clearly people were being discarded. Better to be doing this now, she thought. Whatever penalties awaited the losers up ahead would be spared her, at least for another few days. A perfect time to audition or interview or whatever she was supposed to be doing. And at the least, she was curious. Those who made their way into the workshop rarely came back out. It made her - and everyone else - wonder if the rumors were just that. Maybe the workshop wasn't that special after all? Maybe it was eternal oblivion? Lack of existence altogether? No one knew.

She had seen Santa before, only once. He was strolling through the dungeon where she was sitting with a few girls her age, trying to ignore the leers and sex and gore. She'd thought then, as she did almost every day, that it was a good thing there were no scents in Hell. The blood and sex would have been the worst stench.

Santa did not look like Santa looks. He looked - and

apparently always did in here - like a male model. Yes, he did have white hair, and a short white beard. He was wearing a red suit, sure. But a formal one, a jacket with lapels. He looked like the host of a sex club Christmas party, and he had the presence of...well, of a king. And he moved in spurts, like film that was out of order: you couldn't really follow him with your eyes. He was more than a brain could process. She knew if anyone living saw him, they'd go mad on the spot. You would see him, then see two of him, then see him behind you, then not see him.

Everyone knew not to touch him, not to address him; but no one could put eyes anywhere else. When it was over, she wasn't sure if she was disappointed or relieved. First-year rules didn't apply to him - she didn't want to catch his eye. But now, she'd have to.

The workshop was accessible from anywhere in Hell, so it didn't take long for her to arrive. Sadie remembered her living rituals while preparing for seduction. Here, there was no makeup or hair gel, no perfume, no low-cut tops and high-cut bottoms. That prep time had also steadied her mind; now she had nothing but her eternal youth. She shook herself out like a dog after a bath, combed her hair with her fingers, and approached the line.

The entrance was simply a never-ending black curtain, in front of which stood several beautiful people of all colors and ages. There were always crowds close by, come just to look at them, jerk off, whatever. Sadie pushed her way through the gawkers and approached the one who she thought she'd best charm: a young man only a couple inches above her 5'8".

"I'm here for a job," she said.

"What can you do?" he replied, looking her up and down.

Not the time to downplay herself. "Whatever you need," she said.

"Right answer," said a woman from behind her. "But you might wish you'd never offered."

"Doubt it," Sadie said, jerking up her chin to the much taller olive-skinned beauty.

"Follow me, brave girl," said the woman. As Sadie turned away from the young man, he winked at her. It wasn't conspiratorial; it conveyed he knew something she didn't. Sadie felt distinctly unsafe. Surely, surely, there were things worse than death.

"There are several paths you could audition for," continued the woman, stopping down a long hallway with no demarcations. "They are," she continued with an eyeroll, "boringly predictable. The seven sins." She turned, finally, to face Sadie, ticking them off on her hands. "Vanity. We wear clothes in here, jewelry, tattoo our bodies daily. Designers, artists. Beauty is created." Olive waved her hand, and Sadie could tell she suddenly had makeup on and tame hair.

A second finger counted. "Greed. Treasure, exorbitance. Material things, all you're not supposed to want while living. Extra points if you watch others suffer while you get it." Olive produced a sky blue gem, and inserted it into Sadie's belly button. "The hotter the color, the more the maker endured while producing it." Olive's gem was a yellowish-green. She leaned in close to Sadie's ear. "That's why Santa wears red." Sadie knew she looked like a frightened child - she *was* a frightened child, compared to the ages of these veterans. Maybe she hadn't thought this through?

Olive counted her third finger. "Sloth. Fucking boring, most of the time. These are the people who make scents for tubs," she sang in a saccharine voice. "Soft blankets. But also, drugs. And addiction. And bliss." Sadie shivered. Drugs were *here*, too? She hadn't escaped them after all?

Olive passed Sadie a pill, and she took it. She'd never taken a drug in her life, but this wasn't life. There was no saying no, and she knew it. She felt calmer in seconds, and wanted more and hated that she did. She watched as Olive went on to four.

"Envy's the one I always forget, because that's just getting outside the workshop and indulging in the petty world around us." She shrugged. "They're voyeurs. It's a personal taste."

"Gluttony is fun, kind-of wrapped in. Everything is excess.

They told you it would get boring, right, all those diminishing returns? Eh, you go back out there, and come back here, and reset." Olive shrugged again. "We also have food in here." She patted her ass. "No calories, no bathrooms. And they call this Hell!"

She went on. "Rage. You fight. Or dance, or sing. Performance of any kind. The entertainers - and sometimes teachers, if you want to learn." Olive came at Sadie's throat like lightning, pinning her neck to the plain wall with a bang. "If you're here long enough, you're skilled at Every. Single. Sin."

"You forgot two," Sadie said with a croak. She didn't breathe anymore so couldn't be suffocating, but she felt like she was, and was scared.

Olive smiled. "Pride is built in - it's the rationalizer." She brought her face in close. "Don't we deserve this?"

Then Olive put her lips to Sadie's. Sadie kissed back - Olive was sexy, and Olive was in charge, and Sadie wanted a job. And as she didn't know how to make art, cook, perform, or any of those other things, this was all the audition she had.

Olive kept her hands on Sadie's throat until the kiss was done, a full minute or so. "I had a feeling," she said with a smile, "that was your sin of choice." She clucked Sadie's chin. "I accept your resume. Follow me."

What followed was so ridiculous Sadie started giggling, and couldn't stop through the whole damn thing. Olive - whose name actually *was* Olive - and the man from earlier (who was called Keane) gave her a real-life, honest-to-goodness purity test. It was oral - the verbal kind of oral - and Sadie figured it was to see her comfort with describing sex and her place in it. She restrained her giggle for the first few minutes, leaned back against the wall, and for the first time felt comfortable in Hell. She forgot she couldn't escape the sudden walls that appeared; she forgot they kept feeding her pills. Maybe, if she passed, she could make her own rules. She knew that was delusional. But she had to believe it, at least for now.

The questions were long - not that she had anywhere else

to go - and after what seemed like hours, they hadn't come up with one sexual thing she hadn't done. Once the checklist was done, they asked her to come up with scenarios, which she was ferociously good at. The scenes she imagined were endless. It was no time to be shy; she elaborated to show off her creativity.

Eventually she said, "Aren't you, um, going to ask me to *do* anything?"

Keane smiled and Olive chuckled. "Oh, yes," she said. "But nobody's gonna be touching *you*. San gets that honor."

"So...am I hired."

"Maybe. First, you have to bring us each to orgasm twice: once with your hands, and once with your mouth. Warning: we've had the best."

Keane chuckled. "On the other hand, we're pretty easy."

In under an hour, Sadie did.

"Ask your questions."

After a movie-worthy montage of food, drink, and clothes, Sadie sat with Olive in what looked like an Italian villa. This did not at all seem like what Hell was supposed to be like. Sadie felt the nag of knowing outside of this, countless souls were being tortured, literally, at this moment. And yet...wasn't life like that too? Wasn't joy occurring at the same time as so much pain? She was having a hard time sorting it out, and the drinks she'd tried to turn down didn't help. She had a feeling there'd be no hangover, either.

Shelving the philosophy for the time being, she asked the main question on her mind. "If I'm honest, it wasn't very hard for me to get here. I walked up, followed you through a hallway, and gave four orgasms?"

"I don't hear a question in there," said Olive.

"Do you take everyone who walks up?"

"No."

"How many people do you reject?"

"Almost all. And let me add, Sadie, you haven't been accepted anywhere yet." Olive gave her a pointed look. "Don't you think it's going to be hard going back out there, after having all this? Those who get this far do suffer the most when they have to leave."

Olive leaned in, smiling. "I like you, Sadie. But I can't deny I'd get a kick out of seeing you thrown back to the wolves. I might even enjoy hurting you myself."

Seeing the horrified look on Sadie's face, Olive shrugged. "Time is infinite and true death is impossible. What seems like never ending torture today - or neverending pleasure today - will be a whole lot of nothing in 24000 years. Have some perspective, Sadie. This is nothing. Every second is nothing."

"Tell that to the suffering ones," Sadie murmured.

Olive put her hand over Sadie's. "You think I was never one of those?"

Sadie met her eyes, and admitted she hadn't thought about it.

"I have been in hell for three thousand years. Before *Christ*, Sadie. Before hell was what you learned it was." She paused and then, "I have only been in the Workshop for seventy-two."

Again, Sadie's horrified look and again, Olive's shrug. "Nothing matters. And *that* means only now matters." She chugged the last of her drink, and slapped the table. "Let's go see Santa."

Sadie said, "You didn't actually answer any of my questions."

"San will. Probably. Maybe." She grabbed Sadie's hand, and led her back through the long hall.

Sadie still had more questions than answers. What were her chances of staying? Was there any gray area between this gluttony and that suffering? What was the difference between this and Heaven? She had the sense none of these answers would come easily; and anyway, the most important question had to be: what was Santa like, and what would he want out of her?

She got precious little from Olive. "San sees everyone that we clear, eventually. I fast-tracked you without training because I see you have a...calling. He'll tell you what you'll need to do to stay."

"What do I need to know before I go in there?"

"You already know it."

Sadie was sick of this. "What does that MEAN?" she cried.

Olive had dressed her in a turquoise sheath the color of her gem, barefoot. It was decidedly unglamorous, something Sadie thought Wilma Flinstone might wear on a special day. "Look," Olive said. "You asked for a place here, you're interviewing to get one. There's nothing to know. It's not like you have to study a company portfolio."

"Don't I?"

"Look," Olive said again, stopping and turning to her. "No one really knows what San wants. It changes constantly. It's foolish to even try to predict him. There is absolutely no preparing for him. Ever." She popped her another pill. Sadie was afraid, so afraid, at how much she wanted it.

"I'm scared," Sadie said.

"Of course you are. There is nothing scarier," said Olive. "Chin up."

Sadie entered a dungeon room that didn't feel cold and drafty, but looked like it should have: walls, floor and ceiling were dark cobblestone. There Olive left her.

She felt she could be upside down or sideways in this cube, and not even know. Already, claustrophobia kicked in: Sadie started to lose track of what gravity was, and where she was stepping. Like the brief encounter with Santa before, the room blinked and shifted, faster than her eyes could process. There was no forward or back; one second the wall was in front of her and the next it was a hall again. What do you do when you can't hyperventilate? What do you do when your body doesn't tell you you're afraid? How do you panic without sweat and heartbeat?

What, exactly, are the fates worse than death? Was this just one?

She kept taking steps, as she was told, through the sometimes-hallway into what looked like a throne chamber, still shifting and skipping time and place. As she entered, solid arms grabbed her and pushed her against the new room's wall.

Sadie gasped - she was breathing! - and looked up. And up. Santa was before her, and he was tall, and broad enough that he covered her own tall frame completely. She couldn't see the room around him, boxed in as she was - and it probably wouldn't have made sense anyway.

So she took in what she could see: no horns, no talons. He was wearing a dark red suit, almost purple, with a silky shirt the color of her sheath open at the top, no tie. His skin was darker than Caucasian but lighter than Olive's; his hair was white, in what Sadie would have called a punk-rock style in the living world. Santa had a trim, stubbly white beard. He was breathtakingly beautiful. But what both enticed and destroyed her most were his eyes. Both iris and pupil were black -- black-as-a-black-hole black. There was no doorway to a soul behind these. Or if there was, it was a soul she didn't want to see.

Santa wouldn't be so predictable as to have a pitchfork, fire, or bloody bodies about; instead, in the flashes and skips in time, she watched three things happen. Or thought them, and didn't see them? What difference did it make anymore?

Three things, together and apart, there and gone: Shackles up her arms. Age spots and pruned skin. Track marks of heroin needles. All she feared in life, at once. Like a threat. A reminder. It had barely been a second, and she was laid bare already.

"Good," he said, though she hadn't spoken. His voice was velvet, so much the opposite of torture that it scared her even more. "I like to hear what you sound like when you're surprised." Deep, luminous, a voice you want to keep hearing. Addictive. Just what she'd avoided, all her life.

"Good?" Sadie echoed back, not sure what to say or whether to say it.

"I don't like screamers today," he said. "So, good."

He let her go and put her at arm's length. "I'm Santa," he said. "You may call me Santa. Some people call me San. But not you. Not yet. And you are?"

"Sadie," she said, sounding more confident than she was.

"I know," he said. "Just wanted to hear if you would stutter."

All right, Sadie thought she understood the game now. Her every breath was an audition. If his mood changed this quickly, there was no keeping up with it - Olive was right. But no screaming. No screaming *today*. She fought not to shiver. She'd never keep up. Her arms were normal, for now. She rubbed them. He smiled.

"Sadie," he continued. "Tell me what you miss most about living." She had realized moments ago that she was breathing, but then she felt his breath, and then she *did* shiver. It was a full-on shudder because it had been so long since she felt breath at all. She realized she missed it. Olive was right: she'd likely have to go without that comfort again. Forever.

"Good," Santa said again.

Everything felt like a trick question. So she said the first thing that came to mind, for better or worse. "The smell of cigarettes."

He chuckled. "That's a new one." Was that good? Bad? "Did you smoke?"

"Never. I hate drugs. But the smell of the smoke meant I was with people I felt comfortable with."

"Huh," he said. She stiffened. She didn't like the idea of stumping Santa.

"Have you ever smelled skin burned by a cigarette?"

Sadie struggled to think seriously - absurd, in this wonderland - and retook a deep breath - breathing felt so good! - before she answered. "I don't think so. Once someone dropped one on his leg but I don't think it smelled."

"Noted," he said. "We'll try that."

"What?"

"Get undressed."

Sadie was close to short-circuiting. You can smell scents in hell? She guessed so, if they were breathing in this place. Burn people with cigarettes? Undressed? Was he ever going to move back and give her space? Was she going to get old here?

This is the Devil, she reminded herself. *The. Devil.* Burning skin with cigarettes had to be child's play. Should she up her game? Truth was, there was no winning this game. So she had to go with the only thing she had: Truth. Sadie reached down to pull up her sheath, able to do so without touching him. Would he be burning hot to the touch? Cold as ice? Addictive? Other than Olive's hand, she'd felt no one here. Was Olive warm? Icy? She couldn't remember. All she remembered was the pills, and her breathing. Which was more and more shallow, as her still-young hands pulled at her fabric.

As soon as the sheath reached the top of her head, Santa turned his back and walked across the room. Not considering her nakedness - Sadie never did - she took in the room itself. The only way she could describe it was...colorless. The colors she did see were black, white, gray, beige...and everything else had a translucent, empty sheen, still shapeshifting in front of her. There was no processing shapes. The only bursts of color in the entire room were his suit, her now-discarded sheath, and her gem. Even her own body looked muted, like static.

Sadie didn't know what she'd expected, from the Devil's own room, but still she was surprised all the same. Surely this wasn't even his room. But still: there was no opulence, no roaring fireplace. No sadistic tools, no waitstaff. It was...understated. In fact, it wasn't stated at all. It was the opposite of a statement. Maybe she was supposed to be making the statement. She turned her head to where he leaned, against a pile of large, tan-sheer cubes. He looked bored. Was she supposed to be entertaining him?

All she had was Truth.

"Why am I here exactly?" That didn't come out the way she'd planned; her tone was not in the least deferential. She acted like she was in control. With Satan. She flinched after she spoke, anticipating a blow. Or a cigarette burn.

He laughed quickly, a one-time bark, and uncrossed his arms. Then, just like she'd seen in countless horror movies, he hadn't moved but he was in front of her.

"You're here to ask if you can stay, aren't you?"

Why, oh, why did she keep speaking too soon? It was like her own self was spilling out faster than she could contain. Sadie tried to go easy on herself. She was out of practice while trying to keep to herself for a year. Maybe it was his strength, or this room, affecting her. Either way, she heard herself say, "I'm not even sure I want to stay."

Santa lifted his eyebrows, like a father whose child spoke out of turn.

"I mean, I don't even know what it's like here. I only know that out there it's very, very, I mean it's—"

"Hell. It's Hell. Yes, I know what it is."

"I guess I'm saying..." she said as she tried to stop herself and couldn't. "I don't really know that it's not Hell in here, too." It had to be something about this place, or him. She'd had zero impulse control since she entered this room. Impulse control was the key to seduction. She was failing.

Trying and failing to orient herself in this almost-room, Sadie tried to look past Santa. On one of the drab blocks now sat three hypodermic needles. Her eyes flicked back to him. He looked uninterested in them, but smiled, like a friend would, and kept talking.

"I understand sexuality is your best attribute." Santa spoke like a businessman with a client, not as someone standing in front of a naked girl in Hell. It was so absurd that Sadie giggled. He hadn't even looked at her body. Again, he had almost every woman, ever, at his command. Of course he wouldn't.

His eyebrows raised again at her giggle.

She tried, barely successfully, to control her mouth. "It is. Look, I know you've had millions come through here, and I know I - I could try to - I could -"

She couldn't help it; she kept staring at the needles.

When her eyes returned to Santa, Sadie saw one side of Santa's mouth quirk. She'd expected the Devil to smile like a loon. His friendliness was creepier. What did she know about Hell, anyway?

"You're right, Sadie. You *could* try." He looked in her eyes for a long, long time. She didn't look away this time; she didn't feel like she was supposed to. She thought only about her breathing, could think of nothing else. For the first time in almost a year, inhale, exhale. Panting. Hyperventilating. Why was she surprised Satan was omnipotent? That he knew everything that made her recoil?

Sadie then found herself lifted up, until she was above him, though he wasn't touching her at all. Laws of physics didn't apply here, she knew. She'd seen enough savagery on the ceiling to know that much. But his face was even with her pelvis, and she had to admit this was a new position for her. No human could pull off lifting her so easily.

He leaned just slightly forward and licked a stripe up her pussy bottom to top, a light lap, like a tasting. His tongue was rough, like a cat's, and she exhaled at the roughness, the surprise, the contact. She found herself coming back down, even again with his eyes. He stared at her another long time. He seemed to be waiting for her breathing to slow. Then he said, "You can stay until tomorrow." And then he disappeared. The needles stayed. Sadie didn't approach them.

Suddenly alone, Sadie walked back to her sheath. She tingled inside, warm, as if he had coated her with menthol when he licked her.

"That won't go away," said Keane, suddenly at her side. Sadie gasped again, more frightened than she'd been with Santa himself. "When he marks you, you'll stay that way until he's with you again."

"With me? We didn't actually -"

"No one ever does, Sadie. No one has ever even touched him. This is triumphant, for your first time."

"What? What do you mean no one has?"

"He doesn't fuck us. But don't worry. Doesn't mean you'll go hungry. I have work for you to do."

Sadie stopped walking, a little dizzy from being in a place that actually had solid boundaries. This part of the Workshop felt like claustrophobia-light, compared to what she just saw. She rubbed her eyes.

"Wait. Where's Olive?"

Keane shrugged. "She's gone."

"What do you mean, she's gone? Gone where?"

"She's back out there." He watched her carefully as she took his meaning.

"I could show you, if you want. But you probably don't. And He'll show you anyway, I'm sure of that."

Sadie rubbed her eyes again. "Show me what?" she asked slowly.

Keane shrugged. "If you're here long enough, you'll get used to it. That's all I can say. Let's get to work."

The next day, back in the colorless room, Santa was again leaning against the blocks. The needles were there, and the whole place was shifting, skipping as usual. Sadie could breathe in here; but given the shifting walls and her fear of confinement, she felt like she couldn't.

A few things were different about the room today. There was a giant block in one corner that was not blinking. Sadie almost fell while looking at it, because it was so stable when everything else defied her brain. Also one of the blocks was her turquoise color. Santa patted it. "Sit," he said.

She sat on the colored block, already naked. Today she'd come in without her sheath. She crossed her legs on habit.

"Uh-uh. Spread your legs."

As she did, that menthol-like tingling grew stronger. She took deep breaths to calm her nerves and her ache. In here, she could at least *try* to breathe. She gulped deeply, eager for the feeling.

Santa pulled a cube over and said, "If you please me today, I'll smoke a cigarette for you."

Sadie looked down. "Thank you," she said. She wasn't sure what else to say.

"I won't say you're welcome. No one is ever welcome here."

There was no right answer, so she stayed silent.

"We'll do three things today," he said, like a schoolteacher starting class. "In what order do you want to do them?"

"I, uh, I d-don't know what they are."

"Good," Santa said. "I like stuttering today."

Sadie blinked. She was fucked, and she knew it. How did Olive survive for this long? Was "survive" even the right word?

"Good choice," Santa said. "We'll do Olive first."

Of course he could read her mind. She shook her head. All these phrases people threw around, like Fate Worse Than Death, and No Safe Place. This is where they came from. Not even her mind was safe.

"That's right," Santa said while smiling. "It shouldn't be a surprise, Sadie. You've been told since you were a child that I could see you when you were sleeping."

He turned his eyes to the giant cube. Which was no longer a cube, but a cage. And Olive was in it.

The cage wasn't nearly big enough for Olive's tall frame; she was folded up in it. Her eyes were wild, but she didn't fight. It was the hopelessness that most disturbed Sadie. There was no way out. Of the cage, the room, this place. No privacy, in and outside the body.

Sadie looked at Santa, eyes wide. "Olive has the same fears as I do?"

He smiled, his friendly expression unnerving her as always. "Oh, Sadie," he chastised. "Olive won't face her fears. She'll face *yours*."

The menthol between her legs pulsed, and she felt shame at desire while watching her new friend suffer. Whenever she felt a wave of pleasure, the cage got smaller. Was it worth screaming? She did it anyway.

Santa had found the very perfect torture for Sadie. He'd weaponized her pleasure.

Sadie stood, and ran to the cage, running around it, still screaming. She knew there was no lock, no door, but human habit is to try to make sense, to overcome.

Olive wouldn't look at her. It was a comfort in a way, but Sadie couldn't help reaching for her, futile as it was. Sadie's youthful hand - the ones she'd always enjoyed watching while touching other bodies - caressed Olive's knee. Olive keened in pain; Sadie had an orgasm and fell to her knees. They writhed in unison, for opposite reasons.

Then Sadie too curled into a ball. She let go of the sanity she was trying to hold on to, muttering and begging. "It shouldn't be like this," she said. "Touching, who I touch, they always feel good, I want to make her feel good." She stared at her hands. They were shifting to gnarled, spotted fingers. Did she have to choose? Did she have to give up youthful beauty to free her friend?

She could see Santa, walking around the cage, watching them both flinch, a scientist checking data.

"Pleasure shouldn't be like this," she said, glaring at the Devil.

"Do it again," he said.

"No," she said.

"All right."

Sadie sat back, surprised he'd listened to her. For a moment she considered she might have some power here.

"No," he said in her ear, and she jumped. "I'm just bored. On to the second thing."

The block with the needles on top appeared next to her.

"Have you ever plunged a needle into someone before, Sadie?"

Santa's voice didn't sound like velvet anymore.

Sadie was so angry on Olive's behalf that she kept glaring. "You know I haven't," she said.

"Your choices are," Santa continued, "Heroin, Aging, or Permanent Binds. One goes to you and one goes to Olive."

That was too easy. "She'll take heroin," Sadie said. At least it might feel good, for a little while? It was the least she could do, wasn't it?

"And I'll take the shackles, I mean I've definitely had -"

"I didn't say shackles," Santa said, handing her a needle. "I said binds. Here's the heroin."

Sadie didn't bother saying she didn't know how to do this; she was sure it wouldn't matter. She approached slowly, muttering apologies, praying of all things she could ease Olive's pain.

As she approached Olive's skin, the needle disappeared, and she wound up grabbing Olive's thigh to steady herself. As before, Olive screamed, and Sadie climaxed. Sadie gulped in air, and gulped shame with it.

"I could teach you," said Santa from across the room, "to love suffering."

So this was what it meant, Sadie thought, to get an offer from the Devil. This is what it meant, to sell your Soul. She looked up at him from the ground.

"Do it again," Santa said once more.

The needle was on the ground.

Sadie looked at Olive, then looked at Santa again.

Small cage or big cage, didn't matter. Maybe pleasure was all that ever mattered. That's all Sadie was ever good for, anyway.

She didn't even close her eyes. In fact, she didn't even blink. Sadie picked up the needle, and plunged it into Olive's arm. Olive swooned in momentary relief.

Santa was crouched next to her, eyebrows raised. He said nothing, but he knew. He knew what she was about to do.

"Good," he said.

Sadie grabbed Olive's arm, throwing her friend back to pain. While Olive writhed with limbs on fire, Sadie knew better pleasure than she'd ever had in life. It would have been torture to hear her friend scream. But she could barely hear it, over her own moans.

When Sadie's vision cleared, she saw no more needles. Olive may or may not have been there. Sadie wasn't sure because she was paying attention to where Santa again sat. And again, he patted the colored block. The room was no longer shifting.

"Now," he said, meeting her eyes. Again, she tried not to shiver. His impulsivity was fear personified. Sadie retained some shame; but she also knew that pleasure always beat pain. She'd spent her whole life reaffirming it. Her face showed no regret.

"Now," he repeated. Surprise me."

"Sur- What?" She didn't understand.

Santa smiled a little. "Surprise me. Give me something unexpected."

Sadie's mind raced. He might have played this game millions, literally *millions* of times before. What in the world would he not expect?

Well. Sadie knew she made it this far on her sexuality. She was still shivering, with gelatinous limbs from sexual pleasure. But all that, all she was, was expected. What role in the world had no one played for *Satan*?

She rose, now for once taller than he was, and put her lips to the top of his forehead. She kissed him as if she were superior, parental, as if *she* were comforting *him*. He was the same temperature as the room, as if he were the room himself. Maybe he was.

A beat passed. Two. She felt her non-existent heart start to pound. Olive groaned in her cage, but Sadie couldn't find it in herself to care.

Then Santa let out a deep, luxurious chuckle, that morphed into positively intoxicating rumbling laughter. She couldn't help but laugh too, pulled in by his tide.

Sadie plopped back down to her cube, against her own will. "No one," he said, "and I mean *no one*, has ever dared. I haven't been surprised in so long. So long, Sadie."

Sadie looked down, afraid to meet his eyes even though she knew she'd pleased him.

"I am," he said, "as close as I've ever come to thanking someone."

Sadie asked herself, what do I have to lose? And then she mumbled, somewhat reluctantly, the exact sentence he'd told her just minutes before: "I won't say you're welcome. No one is ever welcome here."

He tipped her chin up again. "You stand out, Sadie." He pulled a cigarette from seemingly nowhere and lit it. She was able to breathe the scent in deep, and swooned at the memory, the longing, the life.

"You are going to sit here and watch me smoke this cigarette," he said, "and then you will go." He kept eye contact with her while he smoked; It was terrifying. She knew he wouldn't always be this pleased with her, and she feared what would happen then. Today she was at the top. She had no place to go, in his eyes, but down. Tomorrow she could be Olive.

All she had was Truth. She dared to believe it was enough to keep her here.

The menthol between her legs throbbed; she was addicted, like she always feared. Maybe addicted, even, to others' pain. She didn't know yet, so she just inhaled, and sought pleasure, like she always had.

Sadie took in the lively scent, and thought of nothing else. Not Olive or her suffering, the bloody ceilings outside, the ache between her legs. And certainly not what she'd have to do next time, to stay right here.

At the end of the cigarette, Santa kept eye contact while he took one last drag, then stubbed out the rest on the edge of his cube. It sizzled and let up one last burst of smoke that traveled through Sadie's nostrils and then her bloodstream, ending right between her legs. There was no hiding the surge, not that she even wanted to. He cocked his head; a corner of his mouth quirked up. And suddenly, within the space of one second, her body relaxed as if she'd just climaxed, coming down slowly - but without the pleasure. She couldn't have explained it to her alive self: she was satiated, panting, even flinching a little. But she felt nothing but the release - only relief, no orgasm. It was strangely infuriating. She closed her eyes to reset herself, feeling at once relieved of the aroused pressure and robbed of that fourth climax.

Even with her eyes closed, she heard him: "You can stay." Her eyes flew open.

Santa was gone; Sadie didn't bother to check whether Olive was still there, and if she was suffering. She just didn't care.

All she knew was that the source of her pleasure was gone, and there was not even a hint of smoke in the air.

But she still heard his voice, for two more words.
"Until tomorrow."

PIANO
PARKER JONES

Lisa's hands were shaking worse than ever. At forty-three, the Parkinsons had already destroyed her body. Church hymns which once danced easily out from her were now marred by missed keys and shaking fingers. She'd been playing since she was a little girl. Her mother gave her lessons, and she had taken lessons from her grandmother before that. Lisa still had the same piano at home that they all learned on. Three generations of pianists would end with her. Now she was the only one in town who knew how to play. A couple kids paid her for lessons, but it was something their parents wanted. None of the kids could really feel the music. Not all of them went to this church, and not all were even from Christian families.

The choir director called out to the congregation of Firelight Baptist Church which consisted of only a few dozen people, mostly old couples who Lisa had known for most of her life. There was Mr. and Ms. Gowen, who always smelled like vinegar but were sweet to her whenever she stopped into their country store for fresh produce. The Pratts had four children, all of them were her Piano students. The Hennings never seemed to like her much, but she never knew why. The choir director said, "If you will please turn in your hymnals to page four-hundred-two."

On this particular Sunday morning, she was playing "Precious Memories" which was one her oldest favorites. Her grandmother used to sing it while cleaning up wrapping paper at Christmas. Now, it made Lisa think about how one day her memories could start slipping away just like her grandmother's had at the end of her life. The difference was that Lisa wasn't an old lady of eighty-three, but she was facing the same end sooner rather than later.

Treatment did nothing to ease the symptoms. "An outlier case," her doctors had told her. Her joints felt stiff when starting the hymn, but her tremors grew more intense after she'd been playing for a while.

"Precious mem'ries, unseen angels,
Sent from somewhere to my soul.
How they linger, ever near me,
And the sacred past unfold.
Precious mem'ries, how they linger,
How they ever flood my soul.
In the stillness of the midnight,
Precious, sacred scenes unfold."

As the song carried on, she could feel her control slipping away like a ring down the garbage disposal. She wondered when her syndrome was going to flip the switch and shred her ability to play altogether. It felt like that reality was coming closer every day.

She struggled to keep her black hair from her face so she could read the sheet music. The pages were yellowed and worn with time and love. It was her grandmother's copy from her bench at home. She'd brought it when the director told her what songs they were preparing for this week's service.

After the music was over, she went to her seat in the front pew. The fabric on them was blood red to reflect the blood of Jesus. She looked up at the massive wooden cross on which hung on the wall behind the Preacher, Justin Harvard, or Brother Justin, as he preferred to be called. Dust gathered on the arms of the cross. The thing hung too high for a proper cleaning. She had half a mind to do it herself before the next choir practice, but she worried that she might lose her balance on the ladder.

The sermon was from Job on how the Lord giveth, and the Lord taketh away. Lisa knew that better than anyone. He'd given her music for forty-three years, and now it was Him who was taking it away. She had no money, no other skills to market. Retirement was still twenty years away at best, and she'd never really get there on giving piano lessons alone. Hell, she may never get there regardless. Music was her gift from God and her gift to the world, and now she couldn't give anymore.

Lisa loved playing for people. At every family or church gathering that had a piano nearby, she was first to volunteer to play a tune. It wasn't always hymns either. She was equally likely to burst out into "Hey Jude" by the Beatles as she was "Precious Memories."

After the sermon concluded, Lisa realized that she had spaced out for most of the lesson, but it was one that she knew well. She was supposed to understand that God was testing her with trials in order to give her a chance to praise Him. Wasn't that what she was doing by playing all of these hymns? Wasn't she doing enough for Him already? He was taking away the only way she knew how to praise Him.

She needed to get back up to the piano, but the steps were getting trickier and trickier. She shuffled to her feet and took baby steps to the carpeted stairs which led to the church's grand piano. She put one foot up on the first step no problem, but her other foot dragged on the second. Her toe caught the carpet, and the loss of balance sent her falling.

Lisa fell forward and hit her chin so hard on the top step that her teeth pierced her tongue with a savage accidental bite. Blood ran from it, but she was able to swallow it. She thought about how one day even that might be beyond her grasp.

Humiliated, she stepped out and looked to the choir director, Clint, who was almost assuredly in the closet. He waived his hands, and the choir started singing "I'll Fly Away" A cappella without her accompaniment on the piano.

She ran to the bathroom which was clearly decorated in the eighties and never updated with gaudy gold fixtures and faucets. The water ran pink with her blood, and she tore off a few paper towels to press on her tongue. Her shaking hands could barely grip the towel enough to free it from the container mounted on the wall. Tears welled in her eyes as her best friend, Audrey, came in to check on her.

Audrey was a mousy woman, still in her thirties but who lived like she was in her sixties. She wore denim dresses and had her frizzy hair in a long ponytail like the wife on that reality show about having as many kids as possible.

Audrey said, "Are you okay, sweetie? Everyone is leaving. I locked the door, so nobody else can get in. They'll just have to go pee in the men's room if they have to go so bad."

"Thank you. I don't want them to see me like this." Lisa had to steady herself by leaning on the sink. She wrapped her hand on the mirror in frustration and said, "God damn it. I can't do this anymore."

Audrey had a pained wince on her face at the sound of Lisa's blasphemous cursing. She said, "You really need to watch that, at least while we're still in the building. Besides, you don't want Brother Justin to hear you. He wouldn't want you playing piano anymore."

"I can't fucking play anymore regardless. You and I both know it. Don't kid yourself just to make me feel better."

Audrey took on the stern tone of a teacher that she sometimes used at the library to quiet rowdy and raucous children. "Look. I know you're upset. You have every right to be after what happened out there, but there is no need for that."

"Sorry," Lisa apologized only half-heartedly.

"You know I love you like a sister, and I know you can work through this if you have faith."

"What if I don't?"

"What do you mean you don't?" The very notion of atheism offended Audrey. It shook her as if Lisa had just confessed to murder.

"I mean that there is no working through it, faith or not. This is progressive. It starts with these tremors and falling and ends with me forgetting how to swallow and seeing faces in the woodgrain of the altar."

Audrey was disappointed like a mother would be in a petulant child. She rubbed her cross necklace and said, "Well, you know who to come to if you need someone to talk to or to pray with."

"Thanks, Audrey. Love you."

After everyone else was long gone, the two of them exited the church bathroom. Lisa said, "I really don't feel comfortable driving, do you think you could take me home?"

Audrey said, "Of course," and they both climbed into her Oldsmobile which had been on the road longer than Audrey had been alive. They drove old country backroads to Lisa's house.

It was a small townhouse nestled up to some lovely woods that were full of the dead leaves of autumn. Red, orange, and yellow piled on top of one another to paint a picture on the ground. Trees leaned on one another in the same way that Lisa leaned on Audrey to help her up the porch steps. She didn't even have to ask. Audrey had simply given her arm, knowing that Lisa needed to take it.

Once inside, Lisa sat on her piano bench since it was the first seat in the living room. Audrey went right to the kitchen and put on a kettle for tea. She knew where everything was, being familiar with the kitchen, and she didn't hesitate to make herself at home. Although, the tea was really more for Lisa than herself. Audrey said, "Why don't you go change out of your church clothes and into something more comfortable while I fix the tea." She even took out the scissors from her purse and clipped a dangling thread from Lisa's old, tattered dress.

The water in the kettle was coming to a boil and so was Lisa. She said, "I really appreciate everything you've done for me, everything you always do for me. But I think I'd really like to be alone."

Audrey had her hand to help her up, but she withdrew it. Audrey said, "Oh. Okay, well... I'll just head on home then. You get some rest."

"Thank you, I'll try." She stood on stiff joints and shaky balance and then shuffled to the door to close it behind

Audrey. She watched through the window in the door until Audrey's car was out of sight. She screamed, and so did the steam erupting from the tea kettle. Tearing at her hair, Lisa collapsed onto the hardwood.

Lisa cried for a while in the quiet house. She kept her blue church dress on that she'd worn almost every Sunday for years. Part of her wondered if she kept it on just to disobey her friend. She loved Audrey, but she didn't seem to understand what she was going through. It hurt to be alone.

Sunset came and went, and she sat in the dark at her piano picking at the keys with one trembling finger. When that started to hurt her joints, she stopped and decided to pray. She fell to her knees and begged, "Please God. If you can hear me, please help me. I don't know what to do. I'm so scared and alone. Please let me know you're there." There was no sound in the house except the ring in the air of her dead piano notes.

In all the times she had prayed to God, He had never bothered to answer. Why would tonight be any different? She thought that, maybe, it was time to try praying to something else.

Then, a calamity shook the house. It sounded like something wormlike slithering over the house and dragging something heavy behind it. The books on the shelves rattled and hit the floor with several flat smacks like a toddler's feet.

The thunderous sound was followed by a thud at her front door. Then, the doorbell rang. Lisa rushed to the door the best she could manage, but it still took too long to limp there, and she nearly fell on the way. She looked through the window and saw a squat fat man with a bald head, round rimmed glasses, and a bowler hat. He smiled at her through the glass showing tiny sharp teeth that were nicotine yellow like the old ladies at church who stood outside smoking before going in for service.

Lisa opened the door and said, "Can I help you?"

The man said, "I believe it was you who was asking for my help, Lisa." It was then that Lisa noticed a large red trunk behind him that looked like something out of time. The outside was lined with red torn leather. Two dozen thick nails pinned the trunk shut. There were no wheels or visible means to move it except for a large noose-like rope tied around it. The man held the end of the rope in his hand like a dog leash.

Lisa knew him, and knew he went by many names. She asked, "What should I call you?" God may not answer her prayers, but the devil had jumped at the chance to help her.

"Oh, who keeps track anymore. I'm fond of the old ones myself. Old Scratch sounds good today, doesn't it? Something your grandmother would have said if she were still with us. Rest her soul. May I come in?"

Lisa let him in through the door and he drug his massive trunk behind him effortlessly even though it looked like it was so heavy that it dug into the old stone porch, making pebbles in its wake. Lisa asked, "So, I take it you are here to offer me a deal of some sort?"

Old Scratch said, "Precisely, precisely. But first, you have to ask me for what you want. I think that might be obvious, but I didn't make the rules." He sat on his trunk breathing heavily as if the walk was what exhausted him rather than pulling the titanic trunk.

Lisa considered for a moment. She felt this was her last chance to refuse the offer. She said, "I want you to fix me. Take away my Parkinson's so I can play piano again. Please, help me."

"And I assume you know the price?"

"My soul..."

"Not the whole thing. Just a piece. Yes, a piece. That's all I'll need from you. I have a feeling you will give me the rest before it's all said and done."

"Will it hurt?"

"Oh... yessssss," he said with a hiss that sounded like he was slurping up drool. The notion was so mouthwatering to him that his eyes rolled back in pleasure.

"How does it work?"

"Give me something of your grandmother's. Something religious, something that was dear to her and therefore dear to you. That will be the symbol of the thing, the physical part of the exchange. Just put it in my trunk when you're ready. Think hard, now. I don't think you want to know what happens if you try to give me something that isn't worth it."

Lisa immediately knew what he wanted. He wanted the sheet music. The hymnal with all of her favorites in it that she used to teach Lisa when she was a little girl. She shuffled over to the piano bench and opened it. Inside was the red book with frayed edges and gold type on the cover.

Lisa took it over to the trunk. When she was within a few feet, she approached it with shaking outstretched arms, holding the book out in front of her as if she were afraid to get too close. Old Scratch stood up and smiled again.

When the book was about a foot away from the trunk opening, the clasp sprung open of its own accord. Lisa looked to Old Scratch, who gave her a wink. Lisa took the final step forward, and the trunk exploded open as dozens of hands flailed through the opening as if desperately trying to escape. A weathered hand of a hag with green flesh and a rusted wedding band grabbed her most prized possession and withdrew. The rest of the dead hands followed suit, and the trunk shut and locked itself.

Lisa recoiled in fear, but she didn't fall. No. She ran. She ran, and it didn't hurt. She didn't shuffle; she could walk freely throughout her house. She did a lap to prove it as Old Scratch sat back down on top of the trunk to watch her. His smile was even bigger now, showing just how sharp his teeth really were.

Lisa ran through her house until she was breathless. Tears of joy were in her eyes now, and she went to the piano. Her fingers flitted across the old worn keys just like they used to. The song came to her immediately; it was Beethoven's Moonlight Sonata. She relished in the melancholy music as it filled her house.

Old Scratch stood up, gathered up his rope, and said, "I'll get out of your hair. I don't want to overstay my welcome." With that, he put on his bowler hat and left. The door closed itself as Lisa continued to play.

She played all through the night and into the morning. That

week she cancelled all of her lessons and didn't leave the house for anything. She barely slept or ate, and by the end of it she looked ragged and emaciated. But she had never felt better.

She hadn't talked to Audrey all week, but she called her the next Sunday for a ride since her car was still at the church where she'd left it. Audrey said, "Of course I can, honey. I'll see you in a bit." Lisa put on her darkest black dress as if she were going to a funeral and waited by the door for Audrey to arrive. When she did, she ran to the car to show her friend.

Audrey's jaw dropped in amazement. The last time they'd seen each other, Lisa had barely been able to walk much less sprint in heels. Audrey said, "I can't believe it. It's a miracle! It's an actual God-given miracle."

Lisa said, "God had nothing to do with it, but it is a miracle. I'm healed, Audrey. I can play piano again. It's just like it used to be. I don't shake. I don't hurt anymore. I'm not going to forget."

On the way to church, Lisa thought about why she was going. It felt like it was mostly out of habit. This time might be for a little taste of blasphemy. The two of them didn't talk much, but Lisa was sure to keep the method of her healing a secret from her Godfearing friend.

When they finally arrived, families were marching in as Brother Justin greeted them at the door with his smile of crooked teeth which were the result of having no money for braces growing up. They gave him a homely charm that the congregation appreciated. His eyes widened when he saw Lisa walking up to the church doors which she hoped she could still pass through.

She said to Brother Justin, "I'm ready to play today, if you'll still have me."

"I'd be delighted." He mouthed the word "wow" as he contemplated the miracle he was witnessing. In all of his years of preaching, he'd never seen one. He'd anointed people with oil and tried to pray for healing over the sick dozens of times in his career, but never once had any of them gotten better. He thought that it was still worth doing because it usually made the dying person feel a little better on their way out the door, but he thought the miracles were just for tv.

As the service began, Lisa took her spot at the grand piano. The pews were full, the choir was in place, and Brother Justin sat in his seat off to the side of pulpit. When she began playing, a hymnal did not come out. The song came to her, and it was a dark dirge that echoed in the lofty ceilings of the sanctuary. Her wicked notes filled the holy room and unhallowed it before everyone's eyes.

The sunlight no longer beamed in through the windows. It was as if God had darkened the sky again because he didn't want to watch what was about to happen.

The choir began to chant the many names of the devil, "Belial, Beelzebub, Behemoth, Most Unclean, Satan, Lucifer…" Some of the congregation stood in horror and ran out the doors enraged. Brother Justin stood and approached the piano, ready to jerk Lisa off her bench if he had to.

As Lisa struck a powerful chord, he went tumbling down the steps and cracked his head on the wooden table at the bottom which read, "This Do In Remembrance Of Me." His blood pooled on the carpet to match the fabric on the pews.

The remainder of the congregation was on their feet, and they joined the Black Mass by tearing off their clothes and using them to cover the crosses. Then, they began an orgy. Some were willing and some, like Audrey, were not. It was a writhing mass of bodies undulating atop one another like a knot of snakes or even the hands in Old Scratch's trunk.

Lisa wanted to stop it, but she couldn't make herself stop. It was as involuntary as her shaking had been, a Satanic seizure that went on and on with the beat of evil music. Even though her fingers were starting to hurt, she couldn't help but laugh at how quickly she was paying the price. She knew that the longer she played the more pieces she was giving away. Worst of all, her grandmother's copy of the sheet music for Precious Mem'ries still sat on the piano from last Sunday. She didn't even recognize it as it no longer held significance to her. She'd given it away to Old Scratch.

Lisa played on as she had no choice, and the notes poured from her piano until her fingers bled.

BIOS

Matthew Barron was raised by a dog in the cornfields of southern Indiana. His biological parents helped too. Today he spends his days mixing and analyzing human blood as a medical technologist in Indianapolis. Matthew enjoys writing in different genres and mediums of storytelling. His short stories have appeared in magazines and anthologies such as *Generation X-ed, And the Dead Shall Sleep No More, The Dread Machine, Ill-Considered Expeditions, Roboterotica, Outposts of Beyond, Sci-Phi Journal* and many more. He's produced two of his plays and released three graphic novels: *Temple of Secrets, The Brute* and *Harmony Unbound*. His most recent book is a paranormal mystery called *Buried Curses*, a follow up to 2020's *Waking Terror*. His sword sorcery book *Valora*, Dystopian novella *Secular City Limits*, and children's book *The Lonely Princess* are also available. For more information, visit **matthewbarron.com** or submatterpress.com

Jay Bower is a horror author living outside St. Louis, MO in the forest of Southern Illinois. He spends his time reading, writing, and convincing his wife the dark stories he writes do not involve her. More information can be found at jaybowerauthor.com.

Michelle Cristiani teaches reading and writing at Portland Community College and has a PhD in anthropology from the University of New Mexico. She won the Margarita Donnelly Prose Prize from Calyx Press in 2018 for her memoir of stroke recovery at age 42, and is now working on a memoir on that stroke and the brain surgeries that followed.

This year, Michelle has been published in *SadGirlsClub* and *Apple in the Dark*. She has an upcoming story in the anthology *Crowded House* by Cleis Press, and a poem in *Wingless Dreamer: First Love Anthology*. Previously she has been published in

Awakenings Review and *Verseweavers* (Oregon Poetry Association). She won the OPA's 2015 Experimental Poetry contest, and placed in the New Poet category also.

Michelle is so Pollyanna-level optimistic that she'd find something good even in Hell. You can find Michelle at **heart-pages.com** and on twitter @heart_pages.

Scott Hughes is a Georgia author whose fiction, poetry, and essays have appeared in such publications as Crazyhorse, One Sentence Poems, Deep Magic, Redheaded Stepchild, Entropy, and Strange Horizons. His short story collection, *The Last Book You'll Ever Read*, is available from Sinister Stoat Press/Weasel Press, and his poetry collection, *The Universe You Swallowed Whole*, is available from Finishing Line Press. His latest story collection, *Horrors & Wonders*, is available now. And he promises that he doesn't literally insert himself into all of his stories—for the most part. For more information, visit **writescott.com**

Parker Jones currently works as a fraud investigator, but writes horror and science fiction in his spare time. He received his degree in English from the University of Tennessee in 2014 and uses it to scare the hell out of his readers. He has a Facebook, Twitter, and Instagram. You can find his self-published anthology of horror stories, *The Wrong Side of the Grass*, on Amazon.

Benjamin Langley sets many of his tales of quiet horror in the Fens, a marshy region of the United Kingdom with a rich history of witchcraft and rich folklore. It is an area of secrets, mystery, and creeping dread. Benjamin should know: he lives, writes, and teaches there. His works include the novels *Dead Branches, Is She Dead in Your Dreams?,* and *Normal,* and the novella *The Fen Witch of Goosefeather Split.* Benjamin's most ambitious work yet, the trilogy *Guy Fawkes: Demon Hunter* is to be released across 2022 and 2023. For further information check out his blog:

https://benjaminlangleywriter.wordpress.com or follow him on twitter: @B_J_Langley.

Julia C. Lewis is a book reviewer, editor and writer. Her work has appeared in anthologies such as *Blackberry Blood, Dead of Night* and *Slash-Her*. She was born and raised in Germany, and also currently lives there after spending some time in the US. Her heart belongs to her husband, two kids, and three dogs. Her favorite book genre is horror with a particular taste in indie horror. You can find her at:

www.curiosityboughtthebook.com
https://www.instagram.com/curiosityboughtthebook/
https://twitter.com/curiositybooked

Liam A Spinage is a former philosophy student, former archaeology educator and former police clerk who spends most of his spare time on the beach gazing up at the sky and across the sea while his imagination runs riot. Occasionally, this imagination has been known to spill out onto paper.